*For you
with love.
-Erica*

Rhiannon and the Otherworld
A novel by Erica Speegle

This is a work of fiction. All the characters and events portrayed in this novel are either fictitious or are used fictitiously.

speegle.erica@gmail.com

Cover by Erica Speegle.

Paperback ISBN: 978-0-692-99895-3

Rhiannon

and the Otherworld
Book One

by Erica Speegle

Chapters

Martin Eats Breakfast

Gilly Martin was unlike other fey. In terms of power and magic, he was outmatched at every turn. In the Otherworld, the land of the fairies, they could cast circles around him. However, today, Martin wasn't concerned with that. After all, it was Tuesday, the weather was divine, and he had gone out to Earth for a bacon and egg sandwich. The others couldn't do that, now could they? Not likely! And Martin would rather have a bacon and egg sandwich than all that silly frippery the High Council cherished so much. He whistled as he walked along the sidewalk towards his favorite diner.

Martin loved humans. He loved that they lived in an unforgiving, unsympathetic, and entirely uncreative world, and yet they still clung to hope and invention as though it were somehow natural. They made so many things! They had to, in order to survive. Earth, with its limited magic, was so much more complicated than what his fellow fairies had to deal with. Humans were full of lovable surprises. He loved their cars that roared down the highway. He loved the mats in front of their doors just for wiping shoes. He loved that they put little bells over the entryway to chime when customers came in, just so that they could look up from their cashier's box with a grin and say, "Hi there, be with you in a moment!"

Martin gave the young man who had greeted him a little salute and settled into a plush seat to wait, relishing in the fact that somebody had made this thing. Actually, come to think of it, it was probably made *by* things that had been made. Weren't humans getting just ever so clever?

Too clever by half, he knew the High Council would grumble. Martin sighed. He ignored the sudden wave of malaise that threatened to derail his special treat of a day. Instead he swiped a menu and admired all the option and freedom that humans had. This was just for something as trite as breakfast, yet they gave themselves two full pages of choices to make! The precious little creatures demanded more and more ways to feel powerful in a world that stripped them of everything that resembled true power.

Well, almost everything.

"Excuse me, sir?"

Martin turned in surprise to an embarrassed woman sitting beside him. She was a delicate thing, clothes neatly pressed and hair neatly pinned. She was holding a baby. The smile he gave her seemed to only add color to her flushed cheeks. "Yes?" He chimed.

"Could you… stop humming? Please? At least, not quite so loudly?" The baby was squirming restlessly and making anxious cooing noises.

Martin blinked and frowned, puzzled. Had he been humming?

He hadn't noticed. "My dear, could you perhaps help me... What exactly was I humming?"

"What?" She seemed alarmed now, but Martin pressed her anyway.

"Yes, terribly sorry but I need to know. Could you perhaps recall a few bars? Repeat them to me? It's quite alright, I promise!" Martin added hurriedly before she could move to a different seat. "I just can't seem to recall myself how it went."

The woman stared at him for a moment, and then pointed across the room. Martin glanced over and saw the jukebox, and for the first time became aware that there was music in the air. He listened to a few bars, and beamed. It was all he could do to keep tears from his eyes.

Here it was, the power of Earth. No wonder the baby couldn't sleep. The notes wove together to a near perfect spell, containing all the energy and life of a summer storm. Martin took a deep breath, tasting the music. The notes sparked on his tongue. Yet another reason to come here. Humans could put magic into music in a way that those from his world never could. In a million years, a fey could not make a song with this kind of power. At least, not most fey.

Martin turned to the mother and her baby. She was confused, but had not yet fled which was a good sign. Maybe he had managed handle himself like a proper human, or at least proper enough. Still smiling, he bowed his head to her. "Thank you, my dear. This is certainly a treat."

The woman's brow furrowed with concern but she smiled a little tentatively. "Well, I'm glad I could help…" She was interrupted by the baby pawing at her face. "Excuse me, I'm sorry. Oh, sweetheart, please calm down." The woman begged as the baby's unhappy grunting pitched towards a fretful cry.

Without a second though, Martin crouched on the ground so that his face was near the woman's lap. She flinched back, alarmed, but before she could pull the baby out of earshot Martin began to sing.

There were no words, just a melody. Quiet, it floated just where the mother and baby could hear it over the lightening summer rock and roll filling the room. The notes swept together. They rolled and tumbled, caressing the edges of the mind. It ushered away the anxious energy that had been so painful mere moments ago, leaving soft space behind. There was nothing to do and nowhere to go. This was a time of peace and calm.

The baby's contorted face relaxed into sleep, and the mother let out a sigh that she could have been carrying around for months. The little tune finished, and Martin landed back in his seat like a perfect decrescendo.

"How did you… you're a *very* good singer." She said, smiling at him. With the worry gone from her face, Martin could see her more clearly. She was pretty, with a certain sharp intelligence to her gaze. The rest of the restaurant buzzed on with the happy, free energy brought in by the jukebox. She was able to sit outside of it now. Martin's own magic was stronger than this recording.

He bowed his head to her with a grin. "It's my gift." He said. "Please, call me Martin. Who are you?"

"My name is Rose, and this little love Deirdre." The woman brushed a soft wisp of dark hair off of the baby's forehead. There was so much love in that gesture. The fey felt a soft, pink bubble well up in his chest. Parenthood was beautiful, wasn't it? If Martin hadn't come to the human world, he would've never known what that looked like. He looked down at the baby and the bubble popped.

"Deirdre, huh? That's an old name, isn't it? Very traditional." Martin said, studying the baby. He hesitated. He blinked and looked away, only to glance back. He was snagged on this child. There was something going on, certainly.

He tried to ignore it. This was his holiday, after all, and if he didn't want to work then he wasn't going to. But this baby…

A pressing, dissonant melody began to play in his head. There was something important about the baby. He was here for a reason. Martin knew what the music between his ears meant, and knew that his free time was as good as over, but he stubbornly dug his heels in. It was enough to drive a person mad, being a marionette like this. How long could he fight it this time?

Martin gritted his teeth under his smile and jerked his eyes up to Rose's as she talked. Her words floated on the outside of the music in his head, but he made himself nod as though he processed anything she was saying.

"In fact, it's my mother-in-law's name. Personally, I would've liked something a little more fashionable, but it's a beautiful name. An old family name." She continued, "My husband should be here any moment! He was just parking the car. You really should meet him if you're a musician! Are you a musician?"

"You could say-" Martin began, but was interrupted when a man walked up to them.

In that moment, Martin knew something was wrong, or very nearly wrong. He couldn't say what it was that made him think so. The man walked a little too quickly, fist jammed into his coat pocket. His eyes flicked through people as though he were sorting them. The music playing in Martin's ears picked up its tempo, and Martin's fingers twitched out the warning rhythm on his thigh. *Bump bad-a-bap, bump bad-a-bap;* Keep an-eye-out, keep an-eye-out.

Martin clinched his hand. No! None of that. He could hold out and enjoy his breakfast in peace. The music's petulant crescendo argued that point, trying to drown out the conversation Martin was already straining to hear.

"Hey, sugar!" The man said, kissing the top of Rose's head. "How's Deedee?"

He didn't even look at Martin.

Rose smiled up at the man adoringly. The melody in Martin's head pitched sharp. "She's a dream." Rose all but cooed at her husband, "Baby, let me introduce you to someone. . . This is Martin."

The man turned a gaze like a pair of meat cleavers on Martin. Martin had to struggle not to laugh. He looked like a monkey guarding his prized fruit, bristling with a smile intended to show off how sharp his teeth were. "Martin, eh? The name is Charles, Charles O'Farrell."

Martin silently wrapped his hand around the man's proffered palm and let Charles play the game of trying to crush Martin's fingers in his grip. The human couldn't really hurt him, so Martin just kept his smile in place. Twenty minutes ago, the fey would've found this wildly entertaining. Now, the infernal music was blaring so loudly in his head that Martin could only struggle not to wince at the bass notes rattling his teeth. He was afraid if he opened his mouth the song would pipe out from between his lips.

Rose filled the pause smoothly. "Martin is a musician, darling. Very talented. He just sang us a little something, and I swear, even you might be impressed."

"A music man, eh?" Charlie's smile gritted slightly, but he clapped Martin jovially on the shoulder as though they were old mates. "Well then! We have something in common!"

Martin only just managed a nod.

"Martin, why don't you join us for breakfast?" Rose said. "I'm sure I don't mind being bored over a little shop talk while you two chat. I really think you'll find he's something special, Charlie."

Charles frowned. "Now, Rose, I'm sure that the man has-"

"Absolutely! I'd love to!" The words popped out of Martin's mouth before he could block them, and just like that the music's vice-grip on his brain released. The wave of relief felt so good that Martin visibly relaxed, smiling in spite of himself as he wilted in his seat. He cupped his hands over his face, trying to keep a calm facade. So that was it, then. The game was up. He hadn't lasted nearly as long as he'd hoped.

"You alright there, Marty?" Charles said. Funny, Martin thought, that he could hear Charles wishing him to say no. At least it was true that if Martin was going to be working today, he had a fun job.

When Martin pushed back his shoulders and lifted his head, his smile was so bright that Charles couldn't hide his disappointment. "Oh, I'm dandy, Charlie boy! Just dandy! But I for one am practically starving, aren't you? And boy, what I wouldn't give for a cup of coffee, am I right?"

Certain that Charles would see, Martin threw a wink to Rose.

Charles forced bark of laughter and gave Martin a look that threatened murder. Martin's smile curled deeper. Now that he was no longer distracted, he could have some fun with the chimp. He couldn't wait to hear Charlie sing.

"Ma'am? Are you ready?" The polite young man from behind the counter now stood looking at Rose, menu and silverware in hand. Charles stepped up to take the lead, but Martin couldn't have that, now could he?

"It's going to be three now, friend." Martin said, sliding to his feet like a trombone. "Can you work some magic and make that happen? You're a prince, an absolute prince."

Martin followed right behind the waiter, being careful to keep Rose and Dierdre in his gaze as they went. Charles laid a protective arm around his wife's shoulder, heavy on her slight frame. The music playing in his head had quieted to a background hum, but Martin found himself tapping the persistent drum beat out on his leg again. Keep an eye out, indeed.

Breakfast was every bit as enjoyable as Martin had hoped, even with the additional company. Not even Charles the Grump could ruin the experience of a bacon and egg sandwich. The crisp bacon flaking gloriously in his mouth, the just-runny yolk gooshing over his tongue and between his teeth… for that pleasure, he would've dealt with a hundred of Charles.

As Martin entertained himself with the verbal gymnastics of avoiding those natural questions about where he had come from or what he did with his time, he knew that the timer on his freedom was running low. The music was always there, waiting, and a few staccato notes peeking out of the background hum let him know that it was growing impatient. There were things that needed finding out, and only one way to do it. The waiter took away his empty plate, and Martin steepled his fingers on the table. The look he gave Charles was so serious that even the chimp's bravado quavered for a moment. New, professional Martin was sitting across the booth. It was time for business.

"So, you sing?" Martin asked as though reminding him of the fact. "Sing me something."

Charles' cocky demeanor was back in a heartbeat. He gave a golden boy chuckle and threw a knowing smile to his wife. He clearly got this all the time. "Ah, sorry pal, it doesn't work like that. I can't just break into song like Snow White."

Martin didn't bother asking what Snow White was. It didn't matter. "Well, then here are some instructions for you! Step one, open your mouth. Step two, just do it just like everybody else."

"Now hold on just a second here," Charles said, face falling. He had not been confronted with this kind of response before. "Just who do you think you are?"

"I think I'm a musician. Who do you think you are?" He said. Martin was perfectly calm. Charlie, on the other hand, was turning the same color as strawberry jam and his eyes were narrowed to slits. To Charlie boy, these were fighting words. Good. The more riled up the chimp was, the more of his story Martin would know when the time came. "So, sing me something, Charlie."

"You get a load of this guy?" Charles said to Rose indignantly, but his wife wasn't looking at him. She seemed preoccupied with the runny eggs left on her plate.

"Rose?" He pressed.

She put down her fork with an apologetic, pleading look. "Well, he did sing for us earlier, Deedee and me… It only seems fair. Go on, sweetheart, just show him how good you are!"

"Fine." Charles said, face now bright pink. "Fine! You want me to sing, I'll sing. Who cares if I make a commotion in public, disrupt all these fine peoples' breakfast. Is that what you want? Fine." He took a deep breath, looked squarely at Martin, and started to sing.

Martin saw the music of his soul.

Charlie's voice was beautiful. It was warm, dusky, earthy… like the look of a horse running through a field. There was something about it that would trample you if you tried to fence it in. He was not somebody to be tied down. He was not somebody to be trifled with. He knew who he was. If anybody tried to mess with him, they would learn too, and fast. Martin could see it all in the song, the truth of who Charlie O'Farrell was and would be. It would take Charles five years before he would crack from professional and personal disappointments. When it happened, it would be bad, and nobody would see it coming. He seemed so nice, so normal, they would say, but the hole he would fall into would be deeper and darker than anyone would believe looking at him right now. Nobody would believe it then, either. . . At least, not until it was too late.

Charles finished his song, and the diner filled up with applause. Proud, he gave the room a little wave. His wife kissed him boldly on the cheek. Martin stared. Visions of the future still susurrated in his mind. It was five years from now. It was today. It was hard to believe that what would be had not yet happened. How could Rose could bare to kiss this man? It was still today. It had not yet happened. Martin swigged his coffee, trying to work something around the dry patch in his throat. He could still see the blood, the bruises, the little girl child...

It had not yet happened! He had to remember that. No matter what he *felt* right now, he knew that it was not yet the truth. There was a very narrow path forward, a path where this version of the future did not come to pass. That had to be why he was here. What could he do?

How could Rose smile at him like that?

It had not yet happened.

"So?" Charles asked, smirking. "What do you think of that, eh?"

Martin felt a physical tremor run through his body as he struggled not to lunge across the table and throttle him. His hand clenched so tightly around the mug that he wondered if it would shatter, and if it did shatter he wondered if he could aim it so that the shards flew at Charles.

Keep it together Martin! He snapped at himself, but he did not have time to find whatever 'it' was, much less the wherewithal to hold it in place. If he gave into his impulses it would not help Deirdre one bit. Some small, petulant part of him screamed in protest, but he knew what he had to do. The music was always there, and sometimes it felt like the music knew everything. Even in his sleep, it never fully left him. It was just a matter of giving it the reigns.

It was like flipping off a switch. He could feel his body and his voice in his throat. His hands relaxed around the coffee mug as he laughed jovially. His thoughts were only sound, an orchestra drowning out everything else.

Martin's voice said, "Oh, Charlie boy, I don't know what to think. There's a chance I'm gonna have to find myself a new line of work after hearing that! I mean, really, boy! That was something. Say, do you folks live around here?"

Martin dully watched Charlie's lips move around words he

could not hear. Then Martin's head bobbed up and down, a serious nod as though the information really meant something to him. He was surprised at the feeling of his hand rubbing his chin.

"Listen, I'm not from around these parts, you see, but I've got friends who would love to hear what you can do. No promises of course, you know how these things go, but could I have a calling card? Something so that I can send them your way if they're interested? Really, you've got something else."

Charles looked happy for the first time all breakfast. The look on Rose's face was so bright and hopeful it almost shook the music's hold on Martin's brain. He knew it was hopeless, but he tried to push words out of his mouth anyway, tried to scream *Run! Get away from him! Don't you know what he'll do to you?*

But she didn't. She couldn't. Because he hadn't done it yet, and there was no telling that Charlie O'Farrell's fate was set in stone. Worse yet, none of this was up to Martin. When the music chose a path for him to follow, Martin had to go. He and the music were not one, but they were not two, either. He had yet to win a battle of wills with the song in his head. He could only have faith that saving the girl was part of the plan. Sometimes it was hard not to just take the most expedient route to a solution. It would be easy to rid the world of a chimp like Charlie. Why did he have to play these infuriating games?

They were leaving the table now. Martin let the music walk

him out the door, let it wave goodbye to Rose and Charlie in the parking lot. Their car doors slammed shut, and he wrenched back his mind. He was near bursting with fury.

"You didn't do *anything?*" Martin hissed, only barely caring that he was spitting his words to an invisible audience. The music seemed lilting, playful, mocking. He buried his hands in his curls and pulled, willing the song to come out his head at the roots. "Why? Why did you make me come here and see this if we were just going to walk away? Even you are never as sadistic as all of this, you wretched…"

He froze. There was a weight in his pocket. Hesitant, he slowly reached inside and pulled out a flute. It was no bigger than a pencil. For a second he stared at it, and the set off at a dead sprint after the car that was pulling out of the lot. When it stopped to turn, Martin banged his palm against Rose's window.

She yelped, nearly jumping out of her skin. Martin gestured for her to roll the window down. Charlie looked put out. Martin was not a runner, and he was gasping for breath, but he held up the flute with passion sparkling in his eyes.

Rose nervously shook her head. "Mister Martin, this is…"

"No, no, this…" He interrupted, waving the flute. He took the flute between his lips and played the simplest melody, six quick notes. "This is for you. If not for you, then for Deedee. Alright? Keep it with you. When you need it…" He played the notes again. He saw Rose's s glaze a little but it wasn't enough.

"Really, friend, we have to go." Charles grumbled. He was being pushed to the outer limits of his patience. Martin ignored him, gripping the car door as though he would be able to hold them in place. The six notes piped out again, frantically flying from the flute, and there it was. Rose was looking beyond him, into something else. He had done it. The spell was cast. She would never forget those notes. She would carry the flute with her for the rest of her life and when things got bad enough…

Rose hummed the tune back to Martin quietly and took the flute from his hand. "Thank you." She said. "It's lovely. And I'll be sure Deedee gets it when she's old enough."

"Well, goodbye then," Charles growled. Without waiting for Martin to step back from the car, he sped off.

Martin watched them go. His breath was still heavy, but only from the desire to murder that chimp. He looked at his watch. Time was such a lousy construct. It would be five years before he could do anything else about this. At least Rose and Deirdre wouldn't be without protection. As long as they remembered the song, Martin could protect them.

"Thank you," Martin muttered under his breath, glancing upwards to the invisible spot over the top of his head that he liked to imagine the music occupied. It was easier to think of it that way than recognizing it's home as inside of him. The music in his head had returned to normal. By normal, he really meant shapeless. There was nothing for him to do again so the tune wasn't getting in his way. He was free, at least until he wasn't.

Martin began to mosey away from the diner. It was time to go wait out the next few years, although from the Otherworld he couldn't be sure how long it would really be. It never seemed to line up between here and there. If he was lucky, time would spin quicker in his world. If he was not, it'd be an even longer wait, but that was alright. When he had something to look forward to, Martin could be an excruciatingly patient fey.

Chapter One

Consequences

Rhiannon O'Farrell laid on the grass. She traced the shapes of clouds floating between trees. She listened to the birds jabbering overhead. She thought about her mother. She was near enough to the house that the noise of wind chimes still reached her, and she could imagine her mother's laughter in the sound. It had been years, but Rhiannon still missed her. It still hurt. Maybe one day it wouldn't anymore, but how could she know? She was only fourteen.

Today had been an awful day. She liked to imagine that her mother could've made it better, somehow. Really, if she were being honest, she didn't enjoy imagining her mother much, but she found herself doing it anyway. Rhiannon would have come home early, crying, and her mom would have listened to her side of the story. Mom probably would have told her that it was all going to be alright. She would have made her cookies, or a sandwich, or maybe just given her a hug. Rhiannon was sure she would've done something even slightly comforting, making her infinitely better than Grandma.

Instead, Grandma had put on that tight, hard, disappointed look and stared at her teacup until Rhiannon had wanted to throw herself on the ground. Nobody could wield crippling shame like her Grandma could. Of course, Rhiannon hadn't caved. She kept her feet planted, chin held high. No breakdowns for her. She was proud of that, but it also made her mad. Why did everything have to be so hard? Why wouldn't she just hear her side of the story? If only she and Grandma could actually talk about anything. Ever.

No, Mom would be much easier to deal with than Grandma. Mom would be her friend, her support, rather than some looming guardian determined to keep her on the 'right path.' It wasn't even the punishment that bothered her, honestly. From the moment Rhiannon had balled up her fists, she knew that there would be consequences. She had made her decision accepting that, confident that this was the right choice anyway. It didn't matter if everybody else saw it differently. They were wrong. The grounding was hardly a punishment for her, anyway. It wasn't like Rhiannon had any friends or social events that she was missing out on. A perk of social isolation.

She heard footsteps in the grass, and sighed. Her little brother, Colin, was like a puppy, following her with unyielding loyalty. Even today when she'd been a whirlwind of self-righteousness and slammed doors, Colin's love was unwavering. Grandma had gone to the store, and left Rhiannon's older brother, Bear, in charge, and Rhiannon had almost immediately run outside to be alone. Apparently, Colin couldn't take a hint. It was okay, though. Although she'd never admit it, she softened in the comfort that he had come after her, even when she was acting like this. She was a little too old to tell him he was the best person in her life, but she hoped that he knew it anyway.

But when a young, female voice said, "What are you doing out here?", Rhiannon's stomach spun cartwheels. She scrambled up off the ground, trying for once in her life not to be all elbows and knees and only succeeding in nearly tipping over the other direction.

Colin was there, alright, standing sheepishly beside the last person Rhiannon thought she would ever see in her backyard. Jennifer Gray was, by a simple and unbiased measurement of fact, the best human being in their school. The visceral gut reaction Rhiannon had was made up of embarrassment at the dirt and grass all over her and betrayal that her little brother had lead this Cool Kid to her sacred hiding spot. How could he have done this? She sent a glare his way and immediately regretted it. No, she couldn't blame Colin. It was common knowledge that it took superhuman effort to say no to the likes of Jennifer Gray.

And now someone like that was looking at boring old Rhiannon as though she expected something. Rhiannon realized suddenly that Jennifer Gray had asked a question. She managed an eloquent, "Uh. . . hi. Just. . . sitting?"

Jennifer Gray smiled at her and looked around. "This is nice. I'd probably come out here all the time if I lived over here."

"Uh. . . " Rhiannon managed to blink intelligently. Scrambling madly in her brain for something, anything to say brought up nothing. All the words had evaporated into thin air. Her brain cheerfully offered her pocket lint.

"I mean, I don't live far. Did you know that it's only like, a twenty-minute walk from my place to here? But this little pond is beautiful. And the trees! We don't have trees like this in my yard." Jennifer Gray seemed unfazed by Rhiannon's lack of response. "Can I sit too?" she asked, and before Rhiannon could protest, she sat in the grass beside her and laid back.

This was surreal. After today, it almost made sense that Jennifer Gray would come to her house, but not like this. Rhiannon would've understood anger or sneering derision, but she just seemed so chill. It was as though they were friends, or at least like this goddess of a high school student had ever said more than ten words to Rhiannon. This was wrong. The familiar wrappings of defensive pride lashed themselves around her soft underbelly, protecting her from this unknown oddity. Jennifer Gray dared to come into her yard and remind her of how boring and average she was? Rhiannon might not have been powerful or particularly outstanding in school, but this was her domain and it was insulting that somebody from that ugly world could invade her sanctuary. Maybe Jennifer Gray could get away with acting like this with other outcasts, but she had picked the wrong underling to mess with today. Rhiannon had enough on her plate without any more help from Jennifer Gray.

Rhiannon's face formed a scowl, she took a breath, and she stopped. Her little brother's hand had latched onto hers, jerking her gaze away from Jennifer. He stared at her with an expression of longing. Rhiannon sighed and relented. Colin was like that. She couldn't really say no to him, either.

"I guess you can hang out for a while," Rhiannon said grudgingly, "but you better not be around when my Grandma gets back or we'll both be in trouble."

"Oh." Jennifer Gray said, watching Rhiannon as she laid down beside her in the grass. "Why's that?"

"Apparently you get in trouble when you punch somebody in the face after fifth period."

"Ah. Right. So, because of. . . "

"Yeah, because of that." Rhiannon found it convenient that they were laying on their backs so that she didn't have to look her in the eye. She could imagine her Grandma, the lines around her mouth pruning with unmet expectations. Her stomach churned. Maybe this glorious creature was only here in her backyard because Jennifer Gray, like her Grandma, was deeply disappointed and wanted to see Rhiannon in her sorry state. Well, whatever. Rhiannon didn't care. If Jennifer Gray wanted to defend her awful boyfriend, then fine, but Rhiannon wasn't going to apologize for doing what she knew was right.

Was she?

Rhiannon was sure she'd done the right thing, but deep down she could see how Jennifer Gray might not share that opinion. Guilt was not the right word for the feeling bubbling in her stomach, but she couldn't just sit here without saying anything. There was nothing for it. She had to force the words to come out of her throat.

It was a tangled, tumbling mess. "For the record, I'm not sorry, but I know I probably shouldn't have. . . Well, at least, I know it wasn't cool. I mean, nothing was cool. About what was going on. Obviously. I guess I didn't mean to cause any more trouble, is all."

"What?" Jennifer laughed. Rhiannon could have dissolved into a pool of shame and melted into the dirt for all eternity. Instead, her armor solidified and she went into high alert, jolting up off the ground in a fuming flash.

"Look, I don't care!" Rhiannon practically shouted. She ignored Colin flinching. She couldn't let him make her feel bad right now. "Jennifer Gray, if you came out here to get an apology, I'm not going to because—"

"Whoa! Whoa, whoa, no, that's not. . . I'm sorry, I didn't mean it like that." Jennifer Gray said, pushing herself up. "Look, I just thought it was funny! For someone who didn't mean to cause trouble, you certainly did, but. . . it's okay. It was trouble that needed to happen. I'm here to say thanks, that's all."

Rhiannon stared at her for a long time. "But, I punched your boyfriend."

"Yeah, you did. And I dumped him. And I told my brother what he'd been doing, and my brother threatened to punch him again if he ever so much as talked to me. I told him to teach me how to throw a punch, too, because seriously? I don't know if I've ever seen anything so cool as what you did today."

Rhiannon stared at her. She had heard the words, she really had, but she was still processing them. She managed to say, "Huh. Wow."

Jennifer shrugged and laid back down. "Yeah, I guess."

They sat in silence for a while before Jennifer Gray said, "You called me by my full name. Nobody does that but my Mom."

"Everybody does that," Rhiannon replied without thinking about it and immediately felt awkward. "I mean, most people at school, when they're talking about you. . . It's like, the way people talk about celebrities. Nobody would refer to Katy Perry as just 'Katy,' right?"

"But I'm not a celebrity. *People* should just call me Jenny." Jennifer retorted, with a look that was both skeptical and stern. She said more with her eyebrows than most people did in ten minute speeches.

"Alright, alright." Rhiannon said, trying to wiggle out from under that look with as casual of a tone as she could manage.

"So, when is your grandma supposed to get home, anyway? Did she leave you here by yourself?" Jennifer Gray asked. Rhiannon mentally scribbled out the thought of her full name and tried to forcibly replace it with Jenny. It felt weird.

"No, my brother's watching me." Rhiannon said. When Jenny looked at Colin skeptically, Rhiannon couldn't help but laugh at the thought of Colin being the responsible one. "My other brother. The older one. He's in the house, probably spying on us, but I don't think he'd tell her you were here." Rhiannon really hoped that was true. If Rhiannon was expecting Bear to just cover for her, the she would've never risked it, but Colin stared at Jenny as though she were the newest Transformers action figure that he didn't have quite enough money to buy. Bear was a pushover for Colin. They all were. Rhiannon looked back at Jenny and was surprised to see her smiling back, as though she had heard every thought.

"Brothers, right?" Jenny laughed, and Rhiannon found herself laughing with her. It felt good to be sharing a friendly moment with Jennifer Gray, who had just told her to call her Jenny. Fairy tales about princesses and bog monsters curled through her brain, but Rhiannon pushed away the image of herself as a slimy, toady beast. Jenny wasn't looking at her that way. Maybe everything was fine. The three kids sat together, looking up at the clouds. It was peaceful.

Jenny broke the silence. "I think I'd like to get to know you, Rhiannon O'Farrell."

They all jumped at the sound of the backdoor slamming. Bear came sprinting across the huge backyard towards them, and Rhiannon's stomach sank. "Great. . ." Rhiannon muttered, and before Bear reached them, she grabbed Jenny's hand and pulled her to her feet. "I'm sorry about this, but you've got go. Like, right now."

Jenny gave the briefest salute before setting off at a dead sprint towards the opposite side of the yard. Her long, beautifully brown legs flew and she scrambled over the fence, disappearing. Rhiannon could not help but be impressed. No wonder Jenny was a track star. Maybe Rhiannon would actually have to go to a track meet now.

Rhiannon balked. *What was she thinking?* Go to a track meet? Over Jennifer Gray? No chance. That was a place for people who had school spirit, wore actual colors, and didn't punch people in the face. No wonder Colin liked her so much. He'd finally met his equal in getting Rhiannon to do stupid things. Today just kept getting more and more bizarre.

When Rhiannon shook her head clear and turned around, Colin was hanging on Bear's arm, trying to feebly to drag him back from where the girls had been sitting. Rhiannon giggled. She'd have to thank him later.

"Colin, get *off!*" Bear groaned, trying to extricate himself with minimal success. Bear was so much bigger than Colin it was comical. He could have probably tossed the kid like a Frisbee, but Bear would never use force with him. His giant hands were so gentle that Colin's twiggy limbs kept slipping out of Bear's grip like minnows. "Rhiannon, tell him to back off, would you?"

"It's cool, Colin, she's gone." Rhiannon said, putting a gentle hand on the top of Colin's fine, soft brown hair. "Thanks for your help."

"Hey!" Bear protested, furrowing his brow at her. "What's the big idea? I'm the one who let her in! Where's my thank you?"

Rhiannon rolled her eyes and sprang on her older brother in a giant, tackling hug that he staggered under. Bear was tall enough that her feet dangled off the ground. "Thank you, Bear!" Rhi proclaimed dramatically. "You are, of course, the best big brother in the galaxy and I love you very much."

"Oh for. . . get *off!*" Bear moaned, struggling to unwrap the arms looped around his shoulders. Colin laughed and sprang up to hang on Bear as well. "Aurgh! Guys, stop! I can't—" He fell under the weight of them, wrapping his arms around their bodies to protect them as they all tumbled to the ground.

Groaning and laughing, the three siblings untangled themselves.

"Well, aren't we having fun!"

Colin was the last to stop laughing. The three of them looked up at the back door and saw Grandma Deirdre looking down at them with folded arms and an arched eyebrow. Bear was on his feet, dusting off dirt and grass before Rhiannon could even manage to get herself fully straightened out. He walked off from them without a backwards glance. In some ways, Rhiannon thought, that was the least surprising and most hurtful thing that had happened today. She and Colin exchanged a look, and he reached out to touch the back of her hand gently. She smiled.

"Thanks, Mouse." Rhiannon whispered, squeezing his hand as he beamed at her, and the two of them headed back up to the house together. She could always count on Colin.

"So, who was your friend?" Grandma Deedee asked, her question punctuated by the door closing a little too hard behind Rhiannon. Of course, Bear had told, the snitch!

"And Bear didn't tell me, so don't go being mad at him." Grandma added. It was unnerving how she could do that.

Grandma had walked to the kitchen. Rhiannon knew she was supposed to follow her in there. For a wild moment, her imagination suggested instead sprinting out to the car and hotwiring it to escape forever, but the aftermath of that decision resembled an apocalyptic death storm she was not prepared to deal with. She waved Collin off and went to face their grandmother.

"Her name is Jennifer. I mean, Jenny! Well. . . She's Jennifer Gray." Rhi said. This would take some getting used to.

Somehow Grandma had already started tidying the kitchen. Nobody tidied like Grandma did, which was good, because if Grandma's unbridled habit for collecting existed without an equally boundless capacity for tidying up, they would not have been able to find the front door. As it was, although every inch of windowsill and countertop had something occupying it, there was never any dust and they never had any pest problems. How she had the energy for it, Rhiannon didn't know. Grandma was tackling the dishes in the sink now. Without being asked, Rhiannon started drying them.

"And you just forgot that you were grounded?" Grandma asked. The question made Rhi's ears burn.

"No. I'm sorry. . . " She muttered.

"What would you like for dinner?" Grandma Deedee asked. "We have potatoes."

Rhiannon hesitated. "That sounds good," she said slowly. This felt like a trap. Wasn't she supposed to dive into the silent treatment? Or worse? Rhiannon eyed her suspiciously. Where were the pursed lips and painful disappointment?

"Then we'll do that." Grandma said.

And that was that. Rhiannon couldn't believe it. They left behind the topic of her misbehavior without ever glancing back. For the next few minutes they talked about how their garden was doing, the weather, and the book that Rhiannon had been reading. She felt so relieved. It was enough to make her feel bashful about the way she had thought about Mom earlier, and she silently apologized to the universe for having doubted her Grandma for even a moment.

"By the way," Grandma said as she handed off the last dish and dried her hands. "You're going to take music lessons."

"What?" Rhiannon was shocked. "Why?"

The pause was longer than Rhiannon had imagined there would be for such a seemingly simple question. It made her nervous.

"It's time. You should have a hobby, don't you think? I mean, now that you have a friend." Grandma said simply.

Rhiannon's emotions tangled and twitched at the suggestion that Jennifer Gray was her friend, but she stuffed that mess into a box to deal with later. There was something weird going on, and Grandma Deirdre was just trying to distract her from the weirdness. Sometimes Grandma would get like this. It was like trying to see through the peep hole on a door. You could pick up enough to get a picture of what was happening, but not enough to be sure that there wasn't something around the corner waiting to jump out at you when you stepped outside. Rhiannon loved Grandma, but didn't trust her. There were too many secrets that Rhi could almost smell. She did her best to mask her suspicions as she pushed forward.

"What kind of music lessons?" Rhiannon asked, keeping her voice light.

"The kind where you learn music." Grandma said, giving a tight smile that Rhiannon had learned meant that she didn't want to answer any more questions.

Okay. . . perhaps a different tactic?

"Thank you, Grandma!" Rhiannon said as cheerfully as she could and kissed her cheek. "I'm excited. What do I need to do to get ready? Anything that I need to do beforehand? When will they start?"

Grandma patted Rhiannon's arm. "No, dear, for now just focus on your school work and I'll tell you when I know more."

"Oh. . . " Rhiannon said glumly, remembering sadly that school still existed. It was impossible to fathom what her peers were thinking, so she preferred to just pretend they were swallowed into nothingness when she wasn't looking at them anymore.

"Yes, well, go on and wash up for dinner." Grandma said briskly.

As she watched her granddaughter shuffle out of the room, Deirdre sighed so heavy and deep that it could've shaken the walls. That was dumb. Now she would have to figure out that mess as well. Music lessons? Where had that even come from? She must be getting senile. It wasn't like she understood what to do with Rhiannon, but you'd think she'd have learned not to shoot from the hip by now.

There was too much at stake with that girl.

Deirdre took a moment to look around at the junk cluttering up her life. She certainly did have a lot of stuff, didn't she? Maybe it was time to clear more space and focus on her grandchildren instead. She picked up an ancient, cracked teacup and rubbed the handle gently with her thumb, as though to remove a spot.

A small, nearly invisible hand popped over the edge of the cup and clung to her thumb. Deirdre smiled to herself and gently took her finger out of the infinitesimally light grasp. Ah yes, the shell fey. The reason she couldn't possibly part with her trinkets.

They were everywhere, the little shadowy beings. Indistinct and blurry, they seemed more like living shimmers than actual creatures, but they were real. Even if nobody else could sense them, they were real. Deirdre felt their energy and knew they relied on her. She didn't collect this stuff for no reason. The little half-creatures needed to have a place to nest. Deirdre put the cracked cup back on the shelf. It was a burden, being the only one who could perceive them, but it was one she carried willingly. Someone had to care for them, after all. What would happen to them without her?

Poor dears, they seemed to be really putting up a fight at the moment. She could see them flickering and darting in the corners of her eyes. Deirdre held out a hand and felt their energy sending pinpricks across her palm. The half-starved creatures always got nervous when any of the children were upset, Rhiannon most of all. Deirdre couldn't blame them. Rhiannon's reactions were so visceral that they turned even her stomach. Bear hadn't been like this at fourteen, had he? Although, of course, Bear was of course his own special situation. The shell did their best to avoid her oldest child. Deirdre would have to do something to calm them later, but for now she had to worry about dinner.

"Bless her, she is so like Bridget," Deirdre muttered as she began to wash the potatoes. In many ways, it was not a bad thing for Rhiannon to take after her mother. But, in the ways that mattered most, it was a big problem. Her daughter was a beautiful, headstrong woman who waltzed into dangerous situations with all of the caution of a tsunami. It was no wonder that Rhiannon was getting into trouble at school, and in many ways Deirdre was just thankful it wasn't any worse. All Deedee wanted was for her grandkids to be safe.

She stopped herself and rubbed her sagging face briskly. No, that wasn't true. She was too old to lie to herself. If all she wanted was for Colin, Rhiannon, and Bear to be safe, then she wouldn't live in this house. She would not let the broken threads collect here like dust. She would not welcome the shell fey into this home and in fact probably would have banned all fairytales and fantasy stories from their bedtime rituals. If she just got rid of all the magic then they would be guaranteed normal lives, wouldn't they?

Or, she could've gone the other direction. She could have taught her kids enough about magic so that if something horrible happened they could protect themselves from it. If she just told them the truth about fairies, about magic, about Martin and their mother. . .

But, Deirdre could not do that. She had tried being honest before, and see what that had gotten her? Pain beyond reckoning. Loss that would have killed a weaker woman. Telling the children was not an option, but neither was turning away the shell fey. The creatures had nowhere else to go, and after all these years Deirdre could no more reject magic than she could saw off her own foot. These truths left her walking a fine line of deception with her most beloved. It was a terrible thing to do, but it was the answer she had chosen long, long ago, in order to survive when it seemed the light had gone out of the world.

The real problem was that Deirdre wasn't sure what she wanted. Things had changed. Of course, she knew who she was and the rules that she had to follow. She was a protector, a title she wore proudly. The problem was that the list of things and people that Deirdre O'Farrell was in charge of protecting was getting so long that sometimes it felt impossible to shield all of them from the myriad dangers she knew of. There was no one to give her answers about these things, either. Nobody had written a parenting book about how to balance magic and the mundane. She just had to believe that she was doing her best, and that if anything truly awful happened, she would be able to fix it alone.

But there was a nagging thought. What was that business about music lessons? Where had that come from?

You know where it comes from.

Without meaning to, Deirdre looked to the mantle, at the beautiful violin hung where a coat of arms or heirloom sword would be, but she closed her eyes and turned back to the task at hand. No. No, she wouldn't do that. If he came to her, well, that was one thing, but to call him? She knew how that would end. He always brought along more complicated problems. She would just have to tell Rhiannon that she had been mistaken. Perhaps she could have Rhiannon take up a sport, instead? It was true the girl could use a hobby. She had been so surprised to realize that Rhiannon had a friend at all that she really hadn't been mad that the girl had broken her punishment.

Deirdre sighed another bone deep sigh as she set the oven to heat. Tomorrow would certainly be a better day. Unlikely that it could be much worse.

All through dinner, Deirdre kept trying to make the children laugh, and she was good at it. She told stories and jokes, made silly faces, and by the end of the meal Rhiannon and Bear were even joining in to make Colin laugh so hard he nearly spat his milk across the table. When she sent them off to bed, she could feel in her bones that everything was alright. The shell fey were calm and full of the laughter they'd shared. Her babies were safe in bed. All was well.

Deirdre began to work on some laundry, her final task before bed. There was always more to do, but there had to be time for rest as well. She was tired.

She blinked. There had been a noise, just a moment ago.

Perhaps she'd imagined it. After all, she was almost falling asleep. Cautiously she continued her task, then froze, hearing it properly this time. It was her. She was humming. What had it been?

You know what it was.

Deirdre closed her eyes, wishing like all the world like she was wrong. She had thought she had forgotten it, but she never quite could. She could still remember the day her mother had taught her to play it with the little penny flute. Deedee strained in the silence for any sign that her fears were correct. She would know soon enough.

Rat-ta-ta-Rat! at the front door.

Although her mind sprang to a thousand different answers besides the truth, there was only one possible answer. Her stomach turned into a cold, hard rock inside of her. She wanted to freeze time so that she could avoid what came next, but life did not work that way. Nothing to do but face it. Her feet followed one after another across the room to the door. Her hand felt every smooth inch of the door knob under her wrinkled fingers, heaved the weight of the wooden slab and there he was.

Martin had not changed a bit in the sixty years she had known him.

"Deedee, my little love!" he drawled, his voice alone sending waves of pleasure and anxiety down her spine. He looked at her with those deep, amber eyes, and smiled so that his whole face seemed to lift an inch from where it normally sat. He flipped his hand, fingers fluttering towards her living room, a gesture she had seen a thousand times and seemed to come straight from her dreams. "May I?"

"Martin," She said. "I knew you'd come."

No doubt you did, Martin thought, glancing around the room. It was a wreck. His skin itched from all of the broken thread that had collected in Deirdre's house. It was like an impossible, kaleidoscopic spider had taken up residence the place, leaving strings of rainbow webbing floating in the air. He did not shudder as he walked through the door, but it was a challenge. The half-dead shell fey were everywhere, lolling their grotesque forms around in unknowing agony. He recalled that Deirdre had described them as shadowy lights. Humans could not see it, but to a fairy this place was a horrible, haunted graveyard. Martin couldn't bear to tell her the truth.

Besides, he truly did not want to ruin her image of the repulsive pets she kept. Her attachment to them was endearing. If Deirdre could see their tragic, disfigured little faces, Martin wondered if she would be so hospitable to them, and they needed somewhere to haunt, did they not? Perhaps it was all for the best. This was the reason that Martin was the only fey that could travel to the human world. Others that tried? The broken, crumpled, sagging figures that peered out from behind figurines and music boxes with eyes too large for their face were not fey anymore. They were what remained when they'd been severed from their home, starved for magic. They were barely even husks.

Martin looked away from a particularly unsettling, skeletally thin specimen with too many hairless limbs to return to the task at hand. Deirdre had aged magnificently. He resisted the urge to trace the beautiful lines etching her face. This was not the time. It was not a strictly social visit. Still, there was no reason to pretend they weren't friends!

"Shall we have some tea, my love?" He moved towards the kitchen without waiting for her to lead. Martin knew where she kept the kettle.

"Will you tell me why you've come?" She said.

Her tone was like a needle popping his bubble of friendliness. Martin sighed as he lit the stove. She was still ever so business-like, wasn't she? He tried again. "Oh please, it's been years, Deedee! Let's talk of pleasantries, just for a moment. Can't we? Here, let's try it. How's the weather? What's the latest gossip? How are the kids?"

He could feel her bristle across the room. His smile stretched unpleasantly. "Really, now? That bad?"

"Martin, I swear, I don't need your—"

"Help?" Martin interrupted her, the word so lightly said that it was almost mocking. "I'm glad to hear that, little love, because I think you'll remember from the last time we met that I told you I was done helping. It is never good for a friendship to be too out of balance and you will recall, my sweet little Deedee, that you are indebted to me by a margin that is not comfortable for either of us. You have been avoiding me."

The two stared at each other, amber eyes boring into slate-grey ones, until the water began to hiss on the stove and Martin returned to the domestic task of tea-making. He could hear her pulling cups from the cupboard behind him as though nothing had happened. He smiled again. There was something simultaneously comforting and unsettling about how little she had changed inside that aging human body. She was simply adorable.

"So," Deirdre said amongst the rattle of saucers. "I take it that you will tell me why you've come, then?"

Martin sighed, pouring the boiling water over the loose tea leaves and watching them bloom. "Yes, I will. Eventually. Do you want to jump right in or can we at least let the tea steep first? I find a warm drink helps in these situations."

They sat across from one another at the table in silence. Deirdre stared at Martin and Martin watched a portly little shell fey that was staring at the tea leaves. It had one unblinking eye lodged in the middle of its body, but had no head to speak of. Tiny arms and legs sprouted from its shape. At just the right moment, when the tea was perfect, it lumbered over to Deirdre and yanked on her sleeve. It was impossible that Deirdre actually felt it, but she began to pour the tea anyway as though she knew.

"Remarkable," Martin murmured.

"What?" Deirdre squinted at him, puzzled.

"All I mean is that you have a fascinating arrangement set up here, my little love." Martin said simply, removing the strainer from his cup and taking a delicate sip of the tea. It was, of course, sublime.

Deirdre did not drink the tea steaming in front of her, but watched him patiently. It was almost physically painful to have him here in front of her, wearing his perfect smile and looking through her with those infinite, fiery eyes. She could not help loving him. She also could not help how much she hated him. He had given her more than she could ever repay, she knew, but it seemed that he had also taken more than she could ever forgive. Although Deedee saw how he was at the root of everything, it was also impossible to say that any of it was really his fault. With everything that had happened, blame was such an impossible thing to place. She wished deeply that she could stop putting it on his shoulders. However, she could not. Her heart couldn't take it. She still needed to hate him.

"Alright, then, love," Martin finally said with a miserable sigh, "If you're so intent upon cutting to the chase then I will do so. But in five minutes I want you to remember that you were the one who rushed into this. I wanted to be friends first." Martin put down the cup and suddenly stopped laughing. Deirdre recognized the chill in his eyes, where the lilting spark had vanished. There was no room for anything but truth.

He said, "We need Rhiannon. I am here to collect her."

White noise panic pierced up her throat, into her skull, and rang out through her blood. "No." She said. Her heartbeat drummed through her whole being. She could feel her hair standing up on her skin, feel the power inside of her. She imagined what she would have to do to stop him. She would not let him so much as look at her granddaughter.

Martin slowly and carefully placed his hands flat on the table, never taking his eyes off of Deirdre. He was certain that she could not see what the shell fey were doing, but Martin could. He didn't dare to move.

The little creatures had swarmed to her. They hung off of every inch of her, translucent and grotesque. Tiny, bright bits of broken thread floating in the air zig-zagged to their hands, and brandishing these splinters of power like weapons, they screeched at him. Any one of them would have been comical, but all together? These mostly dead fey belonged to Deirdre O'Farrell, sworn to her as their life source, and they were ready to fight him, kill him if they could. He knew that they would push themselves to the death for her, but the only corpse in the room would be Deirdre's. He could not accept that outcome.

"Deedee, listen to me." Martin said slowly.

"No." Deirdre growled, her knuckles turning white on the table. She would not lose Rhiannon. She would not let him take her. She felt lightheaded and invincible. Her teeth grit together so hard that her jaw throbbed. "No."

"You need to hear me out." Martin insisted. "I think we can save Bridget."

In a scuttling wave, the shell fey fled back to their hiding places. The magic they had called down for Deirdre floated free in a gossamer cloud around the her as the old woman's eyes widened with shock. "You're lying," she said, but Martin could hear the hope begging him to defy her.

"My love, I have never once lied to you." Martin said, and this was true. Martin never lied. He could make people believe any number of things that weren't true, but that was not the same as lying. "However, nothing is possible without Rhiannon."

The magic gone from her bones, Deirdre seemed smaller somehow. Martin could see the child he'd met all those years ago, six-years old and sniffling. He saw the pain and turmoil on her face, the conflict that she alone shouldered out of sheer, stupid stubbornness, but in the end, she shook her head. "I'm sorry, Martin. But if Rhiannon goes with you, I have no way of knowing she'll ever come back. I ache for my daughter but a chance is not worth losing my granddaughter for. Rhiannon stays with me."

Martin's eyes turned sad. He cupped Deirdre's hands in his and kissed the wrinkled knuckles gently. "My dear, my love, my little light. . . I'm so sorry. This is neither a request, nor a negotiation. The girl belongs to us. You've already agreed."

He felt her hands tense up, but when he met her eyes he saw horrified comprehension dawning there. She knew what he was going to say, Martin could see that, but he had to say it out loud. If he didn't say the words, it didn't count. "Rhiannon is our payment for contract served. She has never been yours to keep."

The moment hung in the air. Time was pushing forward, but Deirdre was shattered and couldn't catch up. Part of her was scrambling, trying to piece together an answer that would keep Rhiannon out of Martin's world. The rest of her was eviscerating herself for all the steps that had led to this place. Of course, they would want Rhiannon. Of course, this was the price, after all these years. How could she have missed it?

She kept trying to reject parts of the reality before her, pretending like there was a loophole. If Deirdre had not been so old, so blinded by her affection for Rhiannon she probably would've realized it sooner. She could've prepared the girl for what was to come. How could her little girl survive? If this was what she thought it was, then the task they were asking of the child was herculean. Deridre had fought to keep magic out of Rhiannon's life, to create a world where perhaps Rhiannon could be normal. It was a chance that her Mother and Grandmother had not been given. Her granddaughter was so practical and mundane that the Otherworld would chew her up, utterly destroy her, if she could even manage to get there.

. . . If she could even get there. With that thought sparking light through the cosmos, the old woman's thin lips cracked into a grin. It was not an answer to the problem. Martin wouldn't give up. Still, the level of complication it offered was rather funny, at least to Deirdre.

"Martin, you don't want her."

Martin fell back in his seat, shaking his head. "Alright, love, what excuse are you going to give me now? She's too short? She has webbed toes? Really, Deedee, you can't talk your way out of it."

"I don't think I'll have to. Really, you're going to love this." Deirdre said, smiling infuriatingly at him. There was a wickedness in those lined eyes that made Martin squint dubiously. Deirdre took a long sip of her tea, relishing in the way her fairy friend nearly twitched with impatience. Finally, she sat down the mug.

"She can't do anything."

It was Martin's turn to stare blankly. His long, arching brows furrowed deeply. "What do you mean?"

"I mean she's got nothing. Her magic never showed up. She doesn't even know about the Otherworld!" Martin still didn't understand so Deirdre began to count off on her fingers all the things her granddaughter didn't know. "She doesn't know about the shell fey. She doesn't know about the Goddesses, the thread, the Source, any of it. She doesn't know where her mother is. She doesn't know what happened to Bear. She knows absolutely nothing, Martin. Magic isn't real to her. You can't use her."

"How is that possible?" he spluttered, aghast. "She lives here! Her brothers are—"

"I kept it from her! I lied! She thinks Bear has a hormone problem, and to her Colin is just her weird, quiet little brother. She never questions it." Deirdre said, laughing. She shrugged hugely, shedding the burden of guilt and anxiety. Her choices thus far had lead them here, and there was nothing to do but see how the chips fell.

"Deirdre, that's insane. You could've killed her."

"No, that wouldn't have happened. I can protect her." Deirdre said rolling her eyes and taking another drink from the tea. "The shell won't touch her, and as long as you stayed away there was no chance of her falling into magic by accident. The less she knew, the less likely I was to lose her."

The less likely she was to turn out like Bridget, Martin realized and had to stop. This was why she'd stopped calling. The way Deirdre looked at him over her teacup stopped him from saying anything, though. She was laughing and smiling, a paper-thin truce to get through this evening. It would be too easy for things to fall apart. Choosing his battles, he let it slide. Martin made a sound between a growl and a sigh.

"Well, she has to have had some natural contact, though. The shell fey are still fey. There's still magic everywhere in this house. She must've picked up something, somewhere? Just by accident? That's the way of it, always. I'm surprised she's not drenched in the stuff."

"Nope. Not at all," Deirdre said. "I'm telling you that girl is clean. She has gone through fourteen years without any sign of a spark, and at this point I'm not convinced she can learn to channel it. I started when I was seven. Bridget was what, four when she accidentally caught you? Yes, I'm sure you all thought that I was training up another little protégée Druid for you, but not this time. You'll have to look elsewhere."

Martin studied Deirdre, glaring, but grinning in spite of himself. Oh, how he loved humans, this human in particular. Who would have thought that after over half a century she could still surprise him? He ran his fingers through his hair, ruffling it deeply.

He didn't have to coax the music for it to bubble up to the surface of his mind, it was just there. It played a simple duet. Two lines that seemed incongruous, out of time and discordant, somehow creating something bigger than the sum of their parts. It seemed impossible but somehow, it still worked. Perhaps not ideal, but something could still be made of the problem. Whoever said that fourteen was too old to believe in fairy tales?

When he opened his eyes, the suspicious look Deirdre gave him brought his old smile to life.

"Alright, little love," Martin said, "But it's not over yet."

"Do tell," Deirdre said, propping her chin on her hand.

"With pleasure," Martin's voice dripped with sweetness. "In truth, there's nowhere else for us to look. Your family is unique in innumerable ways. Not only are you among the most impossibly stubborn creatures on this planet, every shell fey for thousands of miles comes here to roost. You could travel 300 leagues in any direction without finding a single one, because they all come here to you. You've given them a home, which makes them yours, but every shred of thread comes with them. Wild magic doesn't turn up so easily in the void anymore. That limits the market for potential Druids. Where else are we to look?"

"I wish you wouldn't call this place the void." Deirdre grumbled. Although she'd ignored the rest of his statement, Martin knew that just meant she didn't have a rebuttal. She was glaring at him ferociously.

Martin sipped his tea, his gaze faltering as he said the last of his piece. "Besides, Dee, you can't break a contract with a fey, and the terms have been spoken. Ready or not, she's ours."

"But you literally can't take her!" Deirdre said, eyes screwed up with disbelief. "There's no way for her to cross through the gate if there's no magic in her. You know that. How can you do anything if she's stuck here?"

"Perhaps it's time for her to take up music lessons. I hear it does wonders for the soul." Martin suggested amicably.

Deirdre sat still for a moment, eyes searching the table as though it would have some sort of answer for her. Martin watched the shell fey scurry around her feet making anxious cooing noises, tugging on her shoelaces and pant legs as though that might help make their lady happy. Deirdre seemed to resolve herself and looked at Martin's face coldly.

"Give her all the time you can." Deirdre said.

"It doesn't work like that, Dee. You don't get to make demands—"

"Martin." Deirdre's voice went soft and pleading, and Martin's heart lurched uncomfortably. Oh, this human, this horrible, brilliant human. There was something special about this one. There always had been. He was going to get in trouble for this.

"Alright, alright. I won't take her before she's ready, and I won't tell her anything she can learn on her own. I'll do what I can to keep her safe." He wished that he could have promised her safety outright, but that would have been worse than a lie. That sort of promise tangled the lines of fate. He had already learned his lesson about that.

"And don't tell her about Bridget. Please." Deidre added. She looked wistful.

This was harder. "Dee, you know that I must."

"Just not right away! Just give her time to learn about magic before she hears about what happened. Otherwise she might. . . " Deirdre couldn't finish the sentence, shaking her head as tears tried to squeeze out of her eyes.

"Fine." Martin said, clutching her hand. He could see the logic in keeping the details from Rhiannon on this one, at least until she could hold her own. Knowing the full story would make it too tempting to do something stupid. "I'll teach her first."

"Thank you, Martin." Deirdre managed. She gave herself a moment, just a moment, to wonder if she had made the right choices all along. Perhaps her whole life was some horrible chain of mistakes that could have been avoided if she had just. . . But then the moment was gone. This was today, and whatever she had done in the past couldn't be changed now. She straightened up with her familiar, formal demeanor and began to clear the tea things, taking Martin's cold tea away from him. "You can sleep in the basement." She said.

Upstairs, Rhiannon was tucked in bed but she wasn't sleeping. She was trying, of course, but her mind kept rattling over her day again and again. She always did this. She always jumped in and ended up in trouble because nobody else understood.

Why had she hit him? She could've just ignored it. She could've just pretended she didn't know what was going on. It was more of a surprise that she did know, after all. She had only overheard the situation from somebody who was supposed to be Jenny's friend. If Rhiannon had just pretended like she didn't know, had just kept her head down, maybe that would've been better. That seemed to be what everyone else thought, at least. But what kind of a horrible human would that make her?

A common one, Rhiannon conceded. Lots of people had to know about the pictures, or it wouldn't have gotten around to Rhiannon hearing about it. How many people had heard before Rhiannon? How many people had decided to do nothing? And why had it fallen on her to do something different? There were other people, people actually closer to Jenny, adults who were appointed to stop these things from happening, who should have stood up for her before it came down to Rhiannon.

Rhi rubbed her knuckles with her thumb, remembering the way she had just done it. She had stormed up to him, reeled back and swung. Some hot, violent impulse had taken over and all of the social training that told her not to hit people had gone out the window. In some ways, however mad she had been at him, she had been angrier because nobody else had done anything. Nobody had felt like it was worth it to stop him.

Rhiannon rolled over and felt something in her chest let go. That was it, wasn't it? Rhiannon had acted because the school was full of people who were more prepared, more powerful, and more connected to the problem than she was, but nobody had done anything. And that was the way the world worked. Somebody had to do the right thing. When nobody else was willing to, Rhiannon had to be up for the job.

Chapter Two

Once More With Feeling

"Again."

Rhiannon's fingers froze over the keys. Again?

As patiently as she could manage, she resettled her fingers back in the starting position and started once more. She began, counting in her head, playing the rhythmic chords with the left hand, carefully flowing between the higher notes with her right.

"Again," he interrupted.

"Ooo!" Rhiannon wailed, turning a glare on Martin that should've melted the skin off his face. She slammed wild chords to punctuate, "Again, again, again! Is that all you can say?"

Rather than dissolving into satisfying pile of goo, Martin raised one of those long, condescending eyebrows at her and seemed truly puzzled. "My dear, what would you have me say?"

"Anything helpful," Rhiannon pleaded. "For example! What's wrong with it? What am I doing wrong? Too loud, too soft, too fast, wrong notes? What? Just tell me. If you say again one more time, Martin. . . I can't handle it. This is torture."

The silence stretched further than Rhiannon's furious pride could sustain. She realized that he was puzzled, studying her like an unknown insect. She started to wilt under his steady gaze, but she caught herself. Who did he think he was? Compared to Grandma's disappointment, this was nothing. So, she picked her eyes up from her lap and stared back at him, the haughty tilt of her chin a convincing prop to hide the insecurity she felt.

Eventually, he blinked. That was all.

The basement had changed considerably since Martin had moved into it. There was a bed in the corner now and an armchair where Martin was perched, his legs draped at impossible angles. This piano took up the bulk of the space. There was a myriad collection of other, smaller instruments scattered around the place. Rhiannon was acquainted with many of them. In six months, Martin had taken her through seven different instruments. She'd been at the piano for two weeks and already hated it the most.

"Hm," Martin said. He stretched his whole body with a shudder and unwrapped himself from his awkward repose. He was on his feet in a gesture that was bizarrely graceful, reminding Rhiannon of a time-lapse video of a flower blooming. What should've taken thirty uncomfortable seconds of grunting and fumbling for any normal person took Martin only a breath of time, and his suit wasn't even wrinkled. He was loathsome.

"I don't understand quite what you mean, little love."

"My *name* is Rhi-ann-on." She punctuated each syllable, as though perhaps the reason he kept using those unctuous pet names was because he hadn't properly understood her the first thousand times she'd corrected him.

"No, sorry, that's not what I meant." Martin held up a single finger, as though hushing her. "I should've been clearer, obviously. I can see where you got confused. I know your name, of course, dear child." He smiled with a sort of paternal assurance that made Rhiannon nearly scream.

"What confused me," Martin continued, "was your statement. I don't understand your complaint. What is it that you want to know, precisely?"

Rhiannon breathed deeply through her nose and let her words out in a gush, "I would like to know why I have to play the first thirty seconds of Prelude in E Minor for the seventeenth time today. Please."

Martin's brows furrowed. He squished his face up with his hands, pulling on his lips and cheeks in a way that made him look like someone out of a bad cartoon. He squinted at the sheet music, tapping on his cheeks with his spindly fingers the way some of her classmates tapped on their desk when faced with a test question they hadn't studied for. She found it annoying then, too. Finally, he shrugged. "Well, we don't have to if you don't want to."

"Huh?" Rhiannon managed.

"I mean, would you rather do something else? Is that what you're saying?"

"No!" Rhiannon practically screeched. "No, that's not what I'm saying! I don't care about doing something else. In fact, I refuse to do anything else! I'm saying I will not play another note until you to tell me what the first sixteen times were about. I'm saying that I don't know what I'm doing wrong or where the mistakes are and if you don't tell me I can't *fix them.* Are you sure you're a music teacher?"

"My de-. . . Apologies, of course, I mean Rhiannon. Rhiannon, I can teach you things about music that no one else in the world understands," Martin said. He grinned and Rhiannon wanted to kick him in the shins a little more than she usually did. She was too tired to argue with him, though, and had the terrible feeling that if she tried to, he would somehow win.

"Then Mr. Martin. . . please. Can you please teach me something?"

Martin began pacing, fingers drumming away at his cheeks. Rhiannon found herself wincing in anticipation. She had seen this before. She recognized all the familiar signs from the last half dozen instruments, but she still found herself hoping for a different outcome. It couldn't possibly happen again. Not after switching from the clarinet, the glockenspiel, the trumpet, the harmonica, the drums, and the cello. She willed him to instead say that they were going to play the piece all the way through, and that he was going to actually communicate about how to play piano, maybe even give her something specific to practice at home. Maybe, just maybe, these lessons could stop being a complete waste of her time.

"Rhiannon," Martin said finally, stopping suddenly, clapping his hands like a thunderbolt, "I have a new plan!"

"Really now? Pray tell," Rhiannon said, trying to keep the venom out of her voice.

"You're going to play guitar now."

Of course. She let her face fall into her hands. "Right."

Martin closed the lid on the piano keys and from somewhere he produced a guitar case with gleaming silver latches. They clicked crisply as he opened them, as though the instrument were a professional who had been waiting in the wings for just such an occasion. The guitar had known its time would come. The image of the guitar dressed smartly in a business coat like a recent graduate at their first interview snapped Rhiannon back to reality. She couldn't get caught up in silly imaginings right now. She had to put her foot down.

"Wait, stop. What?" Rhiannon shook her head so her long black curls tumbled in a cloud around her face. "No! I'm sick of this! I really don't want to have to learn a new instrument, Martin. Don't do this."

"Rhiannon, frankly I'm not interested in you learning a new instrument either." Martin said with a distant smile as he tuned the guitar. It sounded like it was limbering up, stretching, preparing for a marathon. "If we're really being clear I actually don't want you to learn piano either, and I'm fairly certain you share that opinion as well."

Before Rhiannon was ready at all, the guitar was thrust onto her lap and Martin's too long fingers were sculpting her arms and hands around it. The grip felt unnatural. "Martin, I don't understand!" Rhiannon groaned, trying to let go of the guitar and push it back to him. "Please, just tell me what we're—"

"Rhiannon!" Martin said, clutching her wrists to stop her motion. His voice was stern, and she stopped moving. "I have told you again and again what we're doing here and I am tired of repeating myself! Please, dear sweet little love, please *Rhiannon*, I need you to turn off your mouth and brain and turn on your ears. I need you to actually listen to what I am telling you. Hear me! Hear this!"

Martin's eyes were actually orange. Rhiannon had never noticed, but now, with his face level with hers and his gaze unflinching, unblinking, all she could think about was how the only other creature she'd heard of with eyes like that had been a fox in a book she'd read once. She found that she could not actually make herself talk. Part of her thought that she should be afraid, but her body was relaxed. Somehow, Rhiannon was certain in this moment that he would never actually hurt her.

He put one of his hands on the top of her head, and his words ran goosebumps down her spine. "Rhiannon. I am teaching you to play."

At the end of the hour, Rhiannon lugged the guitar upstairs. Martin had sat down at the piano and was picking out a tune himself. It was pretty enough, but it grated on her every nerve. What a waste of space. She wasn't sure if she meant the piano or the person playing it. She slammed the door to the basement stairs behind her, closing off the noise. Rhiannon groaned, dropped the guitar and beat her head gently against the wall as though it could make it stop.

There was something about him. Rhiannon could've lived the rest of her life without hearing his lilting, feckless voice ever again, but immediately the image of his serious, fiery eyes popped into her mind, twisting her stomach with conflict. There were moments when the façade fell away and he became so deadly serious that she respected him in spite of all the evidence she had against that point. She hated the foolish twit he acted like, but the person underneath. . . well, him she honestly felt she could trust. There was something real there. She was sure in her heart that Martin was actually a complicated puzzle, with layers of awful and pointless incompetence in the way of something that actually mattered. Rhiannon's world fit into neat, tiny boxes which were not the right size for Mr. Martin. She found herself trying to make room for him.

I am teaching you to play.

She shook her head like a dog with wet ears, trying to rattle the phrase out. His words rolled and tumbled around, but never made purchase to something logical. They wouldn't float off to where she could forget about them, either. It seemed like an abstract and meaningless difference in wording rather than a difference of substance. She wanted to believe there was something more to it, but she couldn't help suspecting that it was just Martin being an idiot again.

"Hi!" Jenny swung into the kitchen with a smile like sunlight. "I thought I heard your dulcet groans coming from in here. How was your lesson?"

Rhiannon turned quickly, stomach pirouetting inside of her. "You've gotta stop showing up early! You know I'm not free until five and my brothers are going to get the wrong idea and think that you're here to hang out with them instead of me." Rhiannon lugged the guitar into the living room, Jenny following her. Rhiannon tried to look put out at her unexpected guest, but couldn't stop herself from grinning to herself. Jenny was such a relief after an hour with Martin.

"Who says I'm not? They're a heck of a lot friendlier than you are, anyway." Her friend said, "What's with the guitar? I thought you were taking piano lessons?"

"Me too!" Rhiannon shook her head and deposited the guitar case beside the couch. "Apparently Martin had other plans."

"Oh good ol' Marty! You must tell me the story as soon as I'm comfy." Jenny plopped down on the couch, making a nest for herself among the throw pillows. "Alright, spill."

Rhiannon marveled at how at home the girl could make herself. After all, Rhi lived here and she never really felt that comfortable, but somehow having Jenny here made it a little better. It seemed like they'd been friends their whole lives. Had it really only been half a year? It was incongruous with the Laws of High School as Rhiannon knew it, but whether she could fully accept it or not, the truth was that Jenny was her best friend. She couldn't imagine life without her, now.

Rhiannon sat in an armchair, settling a little stiffly. "As per usual, I wasn't allowed to actually do anything," Rhiannon said, "But this time I couldn't take it. I snapped."

"Wait, you snapped? What did you do?" Jenny leaned into the story. "You didn't like, hit him, did you?"

"What? No!" Rhiannon's eyebrows dug in over her eyes. "What kind of a person do you think I am? That I'm just going to go around punching people?"

"Hey, in my defense you've hit people before!" Jenny protested. "You have a violent streak, Rhi. But sorry I interrupted. What happened?"

Rhiannon shrugged. "Nothing. He just told me I was going to have to do guitar now. He told me that he was teaching me to play."

"Weirdo." Jenny said, shaking her head. "Like, what does that even mean? Why did you have to stop playing the piano to play music?"

"Right?" Rhiannon rolled her eyes and tried to smile it off, surprised at her own pang of disappointment. She realized then that she had hoped Jenny would just get it, the way she sometimes just got other things that Rhiannon found impossibly puzzling. Without a neat answer, she found that she couldn't put away her sprawling thoughts.

Something heavy and soft thwapped into Rhiannon's face. She yelped, swatting the pillow away and completely losing whatever focus she'd had. Jenny cackled. Colin grinned impishly at her from behind the couch, a second throw pillow in his hand. He was clearly poised for a fight.

"You!" Rhiannon shouted and flung the pillow back across the room at her little brother. He dodged and returned fire. The sneaky little scamp grabbed Jenny's arm from the other side of the couch and pulled her to his side. Traitor that she was, Jenny snatched a pillow from the couch and flung it at Rhiannon even as Colin launched another. Rhiannon shrieked and began collecting ammunition.

Ten minutes later they were exhausted, having gone through the escalations and drama of full warfare in their own home. Jenny reached over and ruffled Colin's hair. "Sorry about the backstabbing, Colin," Jenny said.

"Not that it helped me one bit!" Rhiannon snorted.

"We never agreed to play teams!" Jenny said sweetly. In the end, she had probably been the undisputable winner of the pillow fight among the three of them, having managed to pin Rhiannon and trap Colin with a barrage of throw pillows that would've impressed even Bear, who was of course too mature to participate in such games. At one point he had walked through with a grumbling comment about cleaning up after themselves.

Colin was all smiles as he began to pick up. He was ever the good sport. Jenny stood up to help him. "Your Grandma sure has a lot of cool stuff, huh?" Jenny said to him. "What's your favorite?"

Rhiannon watched as Jenny chattered at Colin. He didn't say a word as she nodded and interpreted his gestures and facial responses with ease. Colin had always been remarkably quiet, and it was common for him to go weeks without saying a word. Rhiannon, Bear and Grandma never had any trouble understanding him, but as far as Rhiannon knew this was the first time anyone outside the family had really been able to follow Colin's silence with this much ease. It was more than enough reason to trust Jenny. Anybody who got along with Colin was okay in her book.

"You know, I can play some guitar." Jenny said, bringing Rhiannon back from her thoughts. "Not a lot, but I know a few chords. Want me to show you?"

Rhiannon, somehow, was not surprised. She no longer viewed Jenny as an impossible goddess who could do anything, mostly because of the single time Grandma had encouraged Jenny to try and cook what ended up as a disastrous dinner, but it was amazing how often there was something that she'd dabbled in. Jenny was an avid reader, YouTube watcher, and hobby sampler. She didn't excel at any one thing, aside from track, but Jenny was just good enough at everything for people to confuse her for super-human. That is, as long as she stayed away from an oven.

"Go ahead," Rhiannon said, gesturing toward the case. "I've never seen your musical side before!" Colin flopped on the couch beside Rhiannon to settle in for Jenny's performance.

"Don't get your hopes up. I never said I was good." As she settled herself, the guitar seemed to fit Jenny's body. She cradled against her like a small child curled on her lap. The strings squeaked slightly as Jenny ran her fingers up them, as though she had surprised them with her touch. The girl turned her eyes to her fingers, took a deep breath, and began to play. The chords fluttered through the air. Jenny's quiet voice warbled out a wordless humming tune, more of a warm-up than a performance.

As the notes came to Rhiannon, something odd began to happen. She could feel them slipping into her ears, rolling down the back of her throat. Rhiannon tried to rub at her ears. The feeling was slimy and unpleasant. However, her vision began to fade and she could not see the room clearly anymore. Instead, it felt like she was watching a scene overlaid on top of her reality. As the notes flooded into her ears, the vision got thicker and richer, until it took over and all Rhiannon could do was watch.

It was like a silent movie that she was living inside, the only sound the strumming of Jenny's music and the mumbled, incoherent sound of her voice singing words that may as well have been gibberish. She was in a house she did not recognize. There was a teenager, her brother, standing in the kitchen, standing around a birthday cake full of candles. Her parents were there. She ran to join them, giddy. It wasn't every day that they got to have cake. The last time they'd gotten a treat like this it had been her tenth birthday, when her parents had taken her to a bakery downtown.

But Rhiannon hadn't seen either of her parents since she was a baby. Suddenly she realized that she did not recognize the people she was staring at. She had never seen them before in her life.

Rhiannon slammed back into her own living room. There was no air in her lungs, and she could not breathe. She flailed out and grabbed Colin's arm beside her, clinging desperately to him. He was real. This was real. Everything was back to normal. She managed to snatch tiny gasping breaths, her body screaming for air. Rhi searched frantically, looking at everything around her over and over again to be sure. The air never quite seemed to reach all the way to her lungs.

Colin whimpered beside her and she jerked back her hand, realizing with horror that she'd been digging her fingernails into his arm. "I'm. . . Col, I . . . " Rhiannon gasped desperately, shaking. She found herself crying, chest rattling with sobs that she couldn't explain. Tears streamed onto her t-shirt.

"Rhi! What's wrong?" Jenny's hands were on her shoulders, firm and real. Rhiannon grabbed onto her wrists, being careful not to repeat her mistake with her brother. "Rhiannon?"

"I can't— " Her eyes were watering. It felt like her face was swelling up. Why was it so hard to breathe? She was scared.

Colin reached over Jenny and put his hands on Rhiannon's cheeks, cupping his sister's face and pulling her around to look at him. His eyes were just like hers, blue-grey and calm, his gaze full of love. His hands were getting wet from her tears but Colin just held her there. She was gasping, hiccupping in air as she struggled not to hyperventilate. All Rhiannon could do was tremble pitifully in her little brother's hands. After a moment, he leaned in close to her and whispered in her ear.

"Breathe," He said, then kissed her gently on the cheek.

It felt like someone had loosened a valve that had been ready to burst. Her lungs began to fill up again. Slowly, calmly, she worked air into her body and felt relief wash over her. She laughed even as the tears continued to roll down her cheeks. Nothing was funny about this, but she just felt so much better. She pressed her cheek into Colin's hand as he stroked her hair with the other.

"Are you okay?" Jenny asked. Rhiannon realized that Jenny had grabbed her hand and was squeezing it. "You're alright?"

Rhiannon squeezed her hand back, nodding. "Yeah, I'm okay. I'm sorry, guys! I don't know what happened. I—" Memory of the unknown family, a memory that wasn't hers surfaced in her brain. Her heart felt like it stopped for a second, so she swallowed deeply, forcing herself to keep breathing, and put it aside. "I don't know what that was."

"Rhiannon," came a smooth voice from the kitchen that made all three children turn at once. Martin stood there, peering curiously at them. "I came upstairs to check on you when I heard the music stop. Are you alright?"

Exactly what I need, Rhiannon thought bitterly, quickly pushing Colin and Jenny away from her. "Yeah, totally. I'm fine. You can go back downstairs," Rhiannon insisted.

Perhaps she'd been a bit too forceful, because Martin's eyes went narrow and suspicious. "Hm. . . You know, part of the agreement with your Grandma is that I make sure you're alright when she's away. I'd hate her to come back from her time at the community garden to find that you're actually unwell. Why don't you tell me what happened?"

"Grandma's at a rummage sale!" Rhiannon retorted, as though this were a good enough reason for her not to tell him about the bizarre episode.

Martin held his smile in place, but did not take his eyes off of her. The stupid girl, she was really going to try to hide it from him, wasn't she? He had been patient with her, waiting for months for any sign of magical connection, doing everything he could to spark something inside of her, and the moment it actually happened she was going to bury it away from him? Not a chance. It was enough to make him scream.

"My dear Rhiannon, that's not the point, precisely," he said, unable to keep the hard edge out of his tone. He saw Jenny and Colin flinch worriedly, although Rhiannon's steely gaze did not falter. Well, it was nice to know that he wasn't completely losing his touch, at least. He sighed through his nose and shrugged. "Well, I'm sure you're quite well, then. Just a bit of dizziness? Nothing to worry about, yes?"

"Sure," Rhiannon shot back curtly. The way Martin's smile curled made her very nervous. What was he doing?

"Splendid! But I did enjoy the music your friend was playing. Jenny, isn't it? Why don't you continue? Let us hear the rest of the song."

Rhiannon stiffened. Colin and Jenny looked at her nervously, and Jenny said, "I'm not sure it's a good idea."

"Nonsense! Rhiannon is fine, isn't she?" Martin pressed.

"Well. . . " Jenny said, looking nervously at Rhiannon.

"Yes. I'm fine," Rhiannon insisted, glaring at Martin. Whatever had happened it was a fluke. She tossed her hair as she turned sharply to look at her friend. "Go ahead, Jenny. Play something. I'll listen this time." *And it will all be fine, you stupid old fox,* Rhiannon added in her mind.

Uncertain, Jenny went back to the guitar and picked it up again. Rhiannon braced herself, although she chided herself for being stupid. She wasn't a child. She knew better. It had been a fluke! Some weirdness because of a bad cafeteria lunch or something. She turned her full attention to Jenny, the noise of the hollow guitar body thumping under her fingers as she got situated, the look of her dark braids brushed over her shoulder. Colin reached over to hold her hand, but Rhiannon pulled out of reach with a sharp look. Colin rolled his eyes at her, but she ignored it. She was *not* being too proud, she just wasn't going to deal with Martin's garbage.

It was faster this time. The first notes from Jenny's guitar poured into her ears and her vision clouded immediately, a new vision appearing. She was suddenly cuddled up to an old woman who smelled like butterscotch candies. Peter Pan was playing on an old TV across the room. She felt so completely safe and content, she snuggled up closer to the woman. The lady, whoever she was, stroked her head gently. Unlike last time, she didn't pull herself out of it. She wanted to stay here. She was nearly falling asleep when the music stopped.

At the last note, she jerked forward and fell off the couch. Like she'd been holding her breath, Rhiannon gasped for air. She was choking and spluttering now, doubled over on her hands and knees as she fought for air. But Martin was there, hands on her shoulders, holding something under her nose. It smelled sweet, gentle, and with every gasping inhale it seemed to loosen the constraints on her lungs. It grounded her, and Rhiannon breathed deeply to try and get more of it inside of her. As her body relaxed with the scent, she recognized it as lavender. In a few seconds, she was able to turn her eyes up to Martin.

He was not smiling. It was the first time since she'd known him that he'd looked so grave. Rhiannon was tempted to feel touched at his concern for her, but there was a louder thought that kept her frozen, eyes fixed on him. He had known, the monster. He had known that this was going to happen to her when Jenny played. Whatever was going on, Martin knew what it was. She needed answers.

"Yes, well. . . in time," Martin murmured to her as though he could read her mind. She did not resist as he pulled her upright and helped her back to a seat on the couch. Rhiannon noticed that Jenny was sitting with her hands clamped over her mouth, eyes so wide that Rhiannon wondered if she'd blinked since Rhi had hit the floor. She looked over to Colin and saw that he was practically twitching, struggling not to lunge to her side as Martin helped her up.

"Guys, I'm fine." Rhiannon said firmly, wanting for all the world for that to be true. She pushed herself out of Martin's arms in spite of the fact that she felt like she might fall over. She had to hold it together. Otherwise the two most important people in her life looked like they were going to explode. "Look! I'm fine. Stop worrying," she demanded.

Jenny shook her head, frozen. "I did that?"

"Jenny, listen," Martin said, and the willowy man was at Jenny's side, gently prying her hands away from her face and taking her gaze to his. "Jenny, it's not something you have control over. You are not responsible for what happened to Rhiannon, not in the least. It could very well just be a coincidence that she's responded like this. All the same, I think that she needs to rest. Would you mind leaving Rhiannon here under my care? I'll look after her until she's ready to go home."

Rhiannon had an impulse to protest but choked it back. She wanted to talk to Martin, and she had a feeling that he knew. If they had to do it in private, fine. "It'll be okay, Jenny. I'll come see you when I'm feeling better," Rhiannon said.

It was the first time Rhiannon could remember seeing Jenny actually panicked and unsure. Seeing Jenny like this made her friend seem incredibly fragile and human, and Rhiannon wanted more than anything to cradle these parts of her from the things make her afraid. Right now, that meant fixing whatever was wrong with her. Martin walked Jenny to the door, leaving Rhiannon and Colin.

"Colin, let me talk to Martin."

Her brother shook his head sharply, a resounding not-on-your-life kind of head shake. Rhiannon gave him a wide-eyed look that threatened to show him how mad she could get if he tried to fight her on this. Colin furrowed his brow at her, eyes equally wide as though to ask if she were seriously going to make him leave her right now.

"Yes! I am! Go!" Rhiannon demanded, pointing to the hall that lead to the bedrooms. He pushed himself off the couch and stormed off. "And don't listen!" Rhiannon added, but she knew deep down that this was probably too much of an ask, even for Colin. She wanted to handle this herself, though. She wanted to keep him out of it as long as she could. He already felt too responsible for her as it was.

When Martin closed the door behind Jenny, he came back around the couch eyeing Rhiannon like she was a baited wildcat with fangs bared. Rhiannon breathed through her nose and kept her irritability at bay as he settled on the couch. "Now, we have some things to figure out," He said, folding his fingers neatly over his knees.

"Look, before we go any further, please don't tell Grandma. I don't want anyone to worry about me." But Martin shook his head.

"Too late for that, Rhiannon. You saw that girl. You saw your brother. And you know your Grandma! You are well loved, and when you are loved people will worry for you." The corner of Martin's mouth puckered as he thought, mulling over secrets that Rhiannon could only wonder at. "However, I'm in no rush to provoke Deirdre's particular sort of protective concern, so if we can solve this without her I'd prefer that as well, but you will admit this is presenting an unusual situation."

"Mr. Martin, do you know what's going on with me?" Rhiannon asked.

"Yes and no," Martin said, hands flying up to mime out a tilting scale. "There are things that I would've said were obvious that now make no sense. I have theories of how these things work, but unsurprisingly, you would be anomalous. I've been doing this for years and never seen anyone like you before, Rhiannon O'Farrell."

Rhiannon could only assume he was going on about her music lessons again, confusing though it was, and she shook her head at him. "No, I don't mean that. I mean, am I sick? It was awful. I stopped breathing and get this horrible loopy feeling."

"That's called vertigo. Awful, isn't it?" Martin interrupted matter-of-factly.

The girl flopped back into her seat and groaned, covering her face with her hands, and Martin took a moment to size her up. She was such a paltry thing, wasn't she? Skin and bones, barely up to his elbow. He would've guessed she was eleven rather than thirteen. However slight she was, though, it shouldn't matter for what Martin had in mind. Magic never cared about the size or shape of a shell, only about the strength of spirit, and Rhiannon had more spark in her than anyone he'd ever seen.

So, what was the matter? With the massive potential she had, where was the magic? He had tried over and over to hear her soul through music and nothing was coming through, but her little friend played three warbling chords on a guitar and all of a sudden Rhiannon was convulsing? It didn't add up. Something was wrong, and there was always the chance that his meddling was making it worse. Normally he would just ask her to sing, but that tact hadn't been working for the last six months. It couldn't wait anymore. He would have to take a risk in the hopes of actually diagnosing this.

"Rhiannon, I'm sorry," Martin said.

"What? What for?" Rhiannon asked, peeking at him from between her fingers, but he had already hefted the guitar into his hands. His fingers found their place and he jammed out three angry chords, singing deep dissonance from his belly, and Rhiannon immediately went limp on the sofa.

Martin licked his lips. He would have to be careful, but with all the music magic floating in the air it wouldn't be too hard. He folded his lips together and hummed. The note shimmered around his mouth. Martin wrapped the magic around his fingers, making a malleable putty that throbbed with the sound when he squeezed it. "There you are," he cooed to the note made solid. Rounding the gel in his hands, he gently placed the ball on Rhiannon's forehead and almost instantly ripped it off, reeling from the shrieking in his ears. The sound had been so harsh, so violent that Martin had thought his eardrums would bleed. What in the world?

Martin carefully squeezed off a tiny portion of the note so that a ball of music the size of a pea stuck to his finger. Rather than placing it onto her skin, he held it suspended above her skin, inching closer until the note reflected the sound again but at a volume that he could handle even if it did set his teeth on edge. His whole body had broken out in goosebumps. What a wretched sound! It was the noise of pain embodied, a wrenching sound made up of all the half-heard things that caused mortal skin to crawl. And this was inside of Rhiannon? He could hardly stand to listen to it, much less dare to look inside the noise, but he knew he had to. He had to understand what was going on. If he didn't, he would never know how to help her.

He took a deep breath, wincing in anticipation. He relished the last moment of peace, then opened himself up to the noise.

It ripped through him. Claws tore at his brain, leaving behind ragged strips and scraps. It was like a million tiny, angry hands were fighting him with everything they had. *"Not yours!"* Came the screaming chorus. *"Go away!"*

He planted his will firmly and held his ground, allowing the sound to wash over him with all the brutality it had to offer. It hurt, but if he allowed the pain to flow through him he could stand it. His eyes were squeezed shut against the onslaught but he had to open them, had to see what he was up against. Who was this? What was this?

When he managed to crack his eyes open just a peep, he was so shocked by what he saw that they managed to uproot him, sending him hurling out of Rhiannon's mind and back into his living room. Martin's whole body ached and his stomach clenched violently, threatening to upheave its contents. He couldn't breathe. Hands shaking, Martin pressed his palms against his clammy face, exceedingly thankful to be back even with the staggeringly impossible task ahead of him.

The shell fey were blocking her magic.

Damn those wretched, vile pests. Damn that stupid woman! And damn him as a fool for not safeguarding against this. Nothing ever was easy, was it? The shell fey made themselves scarce when Deirdre wasn't home, but he could still feel them in the corners of the house. It was all he could do not to begin smashing their collected vessels.

He took a minute to lay on the floor, staring at the ceiling as his body repaired itself and slowed the thudding heart in his chest. Trouble, that's all this was. Of course, Deirdre had to be told, because Martin hadn't a clue what to do without her help. He didn't know how to work with the little monsters. It was a pity because she wasn't going to take it well. Love did funny things to humans, it seemed.

And then it connected in Martin's brain. Even though his exhausted body protested, he pushed himself up and looked hard at Rhiannon. That was what she was fighting against? All of that protection, those walls in her brain keeping her away from magic, and somehow Rhiannon had broken through. His feeling swelled inside of him, conflicted and tangled. He felt anger at himself for not having realized there was a problem soon, grief that she had to hurt so much for the craft, but most of all he felt amazed at her. This Jenny must be dreadfully important, Martin realized. Rhiannon was able to break free with her, in spite of everything.

He quickly flicked the tears threatening his eyes away and refocused. Although this did not change anything about their situation, it just meant that their tactics would have to be completely adjusted. He had to wait for Deirdre. So, he straightened up, snapped his fingers, and offered a what he hoped passed for a reassuring smile.

"You alright there?" Martin asked.

Rhiannon grimaced as she worked her mouth, trying to get the weird, cottony feeling out of it. "What happened?" She mumbled.

"Another episode I'm afraid. I don't think we need to rush you off to any caregivers any time soon but I do think you should go rest," Martin said, helping Rhiannon to her feet.

"Alright," Rhiannon said, too groggy to argue. "but will I need to call Grandma?"

Martin hesitated for a moment and then offered her as polite of a smile as he could. "No, my dear. I'll give her a call. You don't need to worry about that."

Chapter Three

Awakening

The whole way home, Deirdre felt an awful, persistent tingling on her forehead. It was like being aware that something was about to touch her face but it wasn't quite doing so. Focusing on driving was difficult. When she'd pulled into the driveway, it had spread down her nose and across her scalp. She rubbed her face but the feeling wouldn't go away. She scrunched up her nose and shook her face. If only there was time to dwell on such things, but of course there wasn't. There was never quite enough time in the day. She needed to get the new little treasures she'd purchased put away.

At the door, she struggled to get her keys out while holding the large cardboard box, but to her surprise, Martin swung the door open before she could manage it. She arched her eyebrows. "Good timing," She said, then saw his face. "What's wrong?"

"Well. . ." Martin began, then stopped when he saw what she was holding. There were at least ten more shell fey nestled inside of it, clinging to their found objects and snickering at each other. He resisted the urge to growl at them like a dog protecting its territory. "Can't you leave that in the car?" He suggested. He'd thought he tone was perfectly pleasant, but Deirdre glared at him anyway.

"No, I can't. I told you that if you want to stay here, you just have to get used to them," She pushed by him into the house, talking over her shoulder as she began to set out her new things. "You didn't answer my question, Martin. What happened?"

"Really, you already have plenty of… trinkets," Martin finished lamely. At the bookshelf, Martin dared to flick a tiny shell fey off of its perch on a carved candle. It squealed satisfyingly, too round and squat to pull itself up from its back.

"Stop that!" Deirdre cried, horrified. She could see the little patch of glittering shadow rolling helplessly beside the candle that it belonged to. She dropped the box and gently helped the tiny creature back up. Martin rolled his eyes. Deirdre rounded on him. "What are you avoiding, Martin?"

He resisted the urge to pout. It was unkind to call this avoidance. After all, everything was related, wasn't it? Everything came back to these awful little pests.

"All I can say is that you're not going to feel nearly so kindly towards your pets when I explain the latest developments with Rhiannon. Care to guess why she can't do magic, Deedee?" Martin oozed saccharine. He relished in the sudden hesitance Deirdre had, her gaze going from the shell fey to Martin.

"What do you mean?" She asked.

Martin told her.

Two hours later, they stood in the hallway outside of Rhiannon's closed door. Martin certainly wasn't going to knock, but Deirdre wasn't moving either.

"We'll do this together?" Deirdre whispered.

"I'm here, aren't I?" Martin hissed back just as quietly.

"Yes, but you're not going to make me do all the talking, are you?"

Martin's nerves were fried. With Deirdre so flustered, the shell fey were buzzing all over the place and the sticky, awful feeling that came with them was making it hard for Martin to stop itching and even harder to be patient with her. He had chased the worthless runts out of his basement, but they weren't afraid of him when they had Deirdre around. They were insufferable. He could only hope that perhaps this latest development might finally bring Deirdre to banish them from her home.

Martin scratched his arm violently. "Will you knock on the door already?"

"We should've made a better plan!"

"We have talked for ages, my sweet," Martin growled. "What do you need?"

"I don't know what I'm going to say!" Deirdre was already backing away. "How am I supposed to explain this? There's too much. Please, let's go back downstairs."

Rhiannon whipped open the door and looked at the huddled

adults with the kind of nonplussed cynicism that was unnerving in a girl of her age. "Really, you two," she sighed. "these doors aren't soundproofed. Did you tell her what happened, then, Martin? Do you know what's happening with me, yet?"

Deirdre straightened her back, immediately forcing a firm expression, but the embarrassed flush in her cheeks took something out of it. "Rhiannon, we need to talk to you," Deirdre said stiffly. Martin rolled his eyes. The authoritarian tone was not the right one to strike. Clearly this was going to go splendidly.

"I gathered," Rhiannon chimed sarcastically, stepping away from the door and flopping on her bed. "So, come on in. What's up?"

Rhiannon's room was small but carefully curated to fit her tastes. Everything was earth tones and cool colors, no patterned fabric or unnecessary frills. It seemed suited to someone much older than fourteen. Martin quietly sat in the blue computer chair and watched Deirdre standing up tall in front of her granddaughter. There was a lengthy pause.

Enough of this. Martin just shrugged and jumped in. "Rhiannon, your Grandma and I have figured out what's wrong with you," He said.

Deirdre looked at him agog. "Nothing is *wrong* with her!"

"What?" Martin felt like a butterfly trapped under a pin. "Didn't we just…"

"Rhi, darling, the problem is not with *you*," Deirdre emphasized, turning back to Rhiannon as though Martin no longer existed. Martin shook his head in amazement. So much for needing his help, apparently. "Martin told me about what was happening. I feel just awful. I can't help but feel that it's entirely my fault."

"Well. . ." Martin injected, raising a hand to add his thoughts with a wince.

"Hush, Martin."

"Fine." He settled back, more than ready to sit this one out.

"Oh my God, are you two married or something?" Rhiannon sniggered, snapping both of their attention directly to her. Martin's trademark grin erupted on his face as Deirdre's face turned a wonderful shade of magenta.

"Like, seriously," Rhiannon continued as her grandmother struggled for her composure. "If there's something going on, just spit it out. I've thought about it. Yeah, it was freaky but if I have a brain aneurism or whatever, ignoring it doesn't fix the problem. It doesn't matter how things got messed up, we just need to fix it, right?"

This highly pragmatic response only flustered Deirdre more. Martin, beaming from ear to ear, drummed out a delighted rhythm on his knees then sprung to his feet.

"Quite right, quite right! So, you are asking in no uncertain terms to be told exactly what is going on, yes?" Martin said.

"No!" Deirdre spluttered, looking at Martin fiercely.

"Yes!" Rhiannon demanded, giving her grandmother an equally challenging look.

Martin held up a finger and thought for moment, eyes flicking back and forth as he planned his statement. "Fine. Then, I believe that it's safe for me to say that Rhiannon, there is a wall in your brain. Sort of. It grew there as a way of protecting you from the risk of harm, but unfortunately it is causing serious problems of its own. The good news is that it should be simple to remove. The bad news. . . hm. . . "

Here Martin furrowed his brow, suddenly stuck. He looked at Deirdre hopefully.

"My dear, I leave it to you to tell her. I believe that by my previous promise my tongue is tied." He bowed and gestured towards an expectant Rhiannon.

"So, you leave the impossible bit to me, then? Typical of you, Martin." Deirdre said through gritted teeth. Of course, he was keeping his word. He had said nothing about magic, or the fey, or the other-world. Martin did always keep his promises, even with she would really rather him not. It left all the messiest bits to Deedee. She sighed.

"Rhiannon. If we fix the problem and take this. . . wall, I believe Martin said, out of your brain, then everything that it's been holding back will. . . come to the surface."

Rhiannon's dark brows had sunk low over her blue eyes until

they were smoldering, icy beads that pierced into the adults before her. All of this was highly suspect. "So, there's something wrong with my brain? Something blocking the neural pathways or something?" Rhiannon shook her head, dubious. "How do you even know that? Don't you need a CAT scan for that or something? Shouldn't we have to go to a doctor? You can't just sit here and tell me a medical diagnosis without running tests!"

"Deirdre, you let this child watch far too much television," Martin said, folding his arms. "How does she even know about doctors?"

Deirdre ignored him. "Rhiannon… I'm sorry, Martin said it was your brain because it's an easier thing to conceptualize. The part of you that's blocked, it's more complicated. It's your… I don't know how to put it. Martin?" She asked, giving him a look. He required no more prompting than this.

"Her soul?" Martin supplied with a flourished shrug. "Her spirit? Her inner universe? Her portion of Divine Will manifesting its power? Dare I call it her magic?"

"Oh, seriously?" Rhiannon laughed. Religion was such a ridiculous thing to bring up. Next thing they'd be telling her that her chakras were blocked or something. But then Rhiannon saw that Grandma's sheepish face was serious.

"Grandma, really?" Rhiannon shook her head. "Now hold on

a second. That's just. . . silly! You can't mean it. Nobody really believes that stuff."

Deirdre felt a wave of relief that washed all the tension out of her shoulders. Nobody who had felt magic, real magic, could ever say something like that. "There, you see, Martin? Proof. Darling, I'm sorry we bothered you."

"Rhiannon, tell me what you saw when Jenny played her song." Martin interrupted.

It was Rhiannon's turn to blush. "What? Nothing!" She said, frustrated at how quickly the words came out. Trying to play it cool, she shrugged and slowed down. "The living room? I don't know what you mean."

Martin allowed his eyebrow to float up to its peak, asking her to please pull the other now, thank you very much. Rhiannon squirmed under that cool stare and finally groaned.

"Okay, whatever! Do you have to be such a bully about it?" Rhiannon groaned but rambled on. "If you're going to be weird, I guess. . . I saw some old lady's place." Rhiannon ended her outrage in a mumble, shoulders hunched over crossed arms.

"What?" Deirdre burst. Rhiannon looked up, feeling something between fear and frustration. She glared.

"So what?" Rhiannon snapped. "I mean, it wasn't a big deal! She was nice."

"I'm sorry, she was nice?" Martin pressed before Deirdre had a chance to explode and ruin everything. "Interesting. How did you know that?"

"She just was, okay? She was my—" Rhiannon stopped short, eyes frozen in surprise. Her gaze went out of focus as she found herself replaying the vivid memory that had bubbled up during Jenny's song. She had been about to say the word 'grandmother'. Rhiannon had been absolutely certain that the old woman sitting beside her, the one she knew that she had absolutely never seen before, was her grandmother. Realization made Rhiannon cover her mouth with both hands, as though she could somehow put all of the words back if she kept any more from coming out, but from the look on Martin and Grandma's face it was too late.

"You saw Jenny's life, didn't you?" Deirdre said. Her voice sounded soft and sad, resigned as though announcing a death. Rhiannon was sacred to speak, but she managed to nod. Her Grandma looked crumpled and defeated. Rhiannon stared at her, scum swelling in her chest as she watched her Grandma wipe tears from her eyes. The old woman turned her gaze bitterly to Martin.

"Alright, well, look at that, Martin! You were right! As though there was ever an alternative to that inevitability."

"If it's any comfort I take no joy in this," Martin said with a tenderness that scared Rhiannon more than Grandma's tears.

Sitting beside Rhiannon on the bed, Deirdre held her in the sort of long, cradling hug that Rhiannon usually protested against. In this moment, however, Rhiannon didn't want to push her back.

"What is it? How does it work? And can you make it stop?" Rhiannon asked. Her voice was a small squeak, making Deirdre's heart squeeze tight.

"It doesn't work like that," Martin said with a sigh. "It's going to get worse before it gets better."

"No." Rhiannon said, sitting up out of Deirdre's arms. "No, I don't want that. I don't want any of... that. Whatever it was, I just want to make it stop."

"Rhiannon, love, I'm sorry," Martin said, "There's nothing we can do. We have to take the wall out and teach you how to—"

"No!" Rhiannon insisted. Her jaw was set, fear making her eyes too wide for her thin face. "Listen to me, you don't get to do that. I don't want you to! I just want my life to stay normal without any more of the weirdness. I've got enough to deal with without whatever that was."

"Magic." Deirdre said, flinching under Rhiannon's wild, harsh stare. "Rhiannon, it's the only word for it that makes any sense. It's magic."

"You have got to be joking!" Rhiannon was losing control of her volume, scooting away from Deirdre. "No way!"

"Rhiannon! Please don't scream." Deirdre pleaded, holding her hands up as though she could push all of this emotional chaos back into control by sheer force of will.

"Oh, come *on*! You're telling me to be *quiet* when you're sitting here trying to tell me that I'm getting psychotic visions and seizures because of *magic?* This should classify as child abuse! You should have to be committed for being totally insane!*"* Rhiannon barked. She spat her words so fast they were like tiny needles jabbing into Deirdre's heart. The old woman cringed.

Rhiannon saw the pain in her grandmother's face and guilt washed over her, but the hot, needing rage refused to quit. She took a deep breath, steadied herself and met Grandma's eyes squarely. "Grandma, this is the most ridiculous thing I've ever heard. But if there's something in me, something in my *brain* protecting me from all of this nonsense, then I just have to say that you better not touch it."

"Fine." Martin said, drawing all eyes in the room to him. The two women stared at him, the picture of indifference as he had some-how found a way to lounge in the armless rolling chair.

"Excuse me?" Deirdre said, clearly off balance.

"Just like that?" Rhiannon wasn't buying it either.

"Ladies!" Martin sighed, shooing off their disbelief with his butterfly fingers fluttering through the air. "Life is not scripted. There is not one answer. There are, in fact, infinite possibilities. If Rhiannon decides to refuse our help, then so be it. Now she knows what's going on and she's allowed to make an informed decision. She belongs to herself, after all. No other claim can really supersede that most base law. I accept what you've said, Rhiannon, and although it's none of my business, I support your decision."

"Thank you?" Rhiannon tried, still puzzled.

"Martin, are you serious?" Deirdre said, "After all this time you're just going to quit like that? You're just going to leave her, with everything at stake, with your people—"

"Deedee, my succulent pet, we are at an impasse. What choice do I have?" Martin shrugged lightly, and stretched, getting to his feet in his seemingly choreographed way. "My personal stakes in the issue are null at this moment. Rhiannon knows what's at stake for herself, and she's decided that her friendship with Jennifer Gray is less important that keeping her life as normal as possible."

Rhiannon stood, halting Martin's move towards the door. "Wait. Stop. What did you say? What does Jenny have to do with this?" The teen's demeanor had changed. Her fear and anxiety for herself had vanished and the concern in her face was more mature and analytical than before. Deirdre didn't dare to move.

Martin turned back, blinking as though surprised by her question. "My dear... Ah, apologies, Rhiannon. Rhiannon, I thought you'd surely put it together. If your life is going to stay normal without any 'weirdness', so to speak, you can no longer associate with Jennifer Gray. Even the protections that are blocking all other forms of magic… or, should I say, 'weirdness', from your life are not strong enough to stop the outbursts that happen around her. Who knows, though? Perhaps the wards will get stronger in response to the relationship. Of course, your bond will get stronger as well, leading to more outbursts. I seriously doubt that the barriers in your… ahm, yes, *'brain'*, will keep up." He threw in finger quotes for dramatic effect, smiling warmly as she glared.

"But it's not Jenny's fault!" Rhiannon snapped.

"An arguably fair point!" Martin replied, "But here we are questioning the quest of normalcy. Let's say that you decide to maintain your relationship with the Gray girl and keep the wall in your head. You will never learn to actually control the unnamable power existing inside of you which we shall not call magic, but it will simply continue to overwhelm you and leak out in more and more dangerous ways. Without control, there is no telling the damage you might cause. I'm sure you've read at least some fairy tales in your day, even if they are just silly nonsense. The truth is, Rhiannon, that you will never have a normal life if you keep the wall and Jennifer. So, you have chosen the wall. I assume you'll want to tell her you won't be coming to her birthday party, then."

"Shut up." Rhiannon snarled. "Just stop talking and let me think."

As Martin and Rhiannon stared at each other, Deirdre watched. As she looked at the tall, thin fey she had loved all her life and the girl she had cherished for the last thirteen years, she realized that although she knew them both separately, together they were each something new. She had never seen Martin have to try so hard. Although he was grinning and holding himself as though all was well, she was nearly leaning towards him with how hard he was pulling on this moment. Rhiannon was making him struggle.

"Fine." Rhiannon said, breaking the silence with a curt nod. "Do it. Teach me how to be safe, and let me face this head on. But don't you dare be smug about it, Martin."

The tension relaxed from the room and Deirdre breathed again. "Thank you, Rhiannon. I promise we'll figure out a way to make it alright again. I can help-"

"You knew about this? About magic and everything?" Rhiannon asked suddenly, giving Deirdre a glare that stopped her short. Her grandmother hesitated long enough that Rhiannon didn't need to hear the words she said next.

"Not all of it. Not the barrier inside you, but the magic? Yes. I did. I'm sorry, I thought that keeping it from you was for the best…"

Rhiannon sat for a moment, struggling with what she was

feeling. It was too big to put into words, like something had been carved out around her heart and trying to name it was just pouring sand into the abyss. She managed to nod, even though she didn't feel like it. "I get it," Rhiannon said, even though she didn't, and she tried to smile. It felt weak even to her. "I'm sorry for what I said earlier. I didn't mean it, you know."

"I know," Deirdre said, even though she didn't. She kissed Rhiannon dryly on the forehead, but the girl turned her head away from her touch. Deirdre stared at her for a moment, stuck. She loved her granddaughter so much.

"Deirdre, we should get started," Martin interrupted gently, "Don't you agree?"

Deirdre struggled. She wanted to grab Rhiannon by the shoulders and shake her. She wanted to hug the girl and hold onto her until Rhiannon knew it really was okay. She wanted to sit for hours and tell the girl everything.

But that conversation was so much heavier than either of them could take.

"Alright," Deidre said, standing from the bed. "but they're particular. Normally I can get a few of them whenever I ask, but to be sure that all of them are here and on board we're going to need special arrangements. Rhiannon, for right now, just try to relax. Martin, please go fetch as many candles as you can find. They tend to like firelight. While you're at it, bring up the violin."

Martin left without a word and Deirdre knelt on the floor, closing her eyes and breathing deeply. Rhiannon hesitated to interrupt her. She pushed aside the questions she had about who Grandma was talking about and what was going to happen next, but one question would not sit still. "Um… Grandma? Why do we need the violin?"

Deirdre had a clear, sudden flash of a day long before Rhiannon or Bridget had been born. She opened her eyes, smiling at Rhiannon. "That, my dear girl, is a very old story." Deirdre sighed. The day when Martin had arrived with that violin should've scared Deirdre off of magic for the rest of time, but when he had burst into the room, brandishing the bow like a sword… That moment of fire and fury had ignited something in her that still burned today. She wondered if today would change Rhiannon in the same ways. Deirdre reached out and squeezed her granddaughter's knee gently.

"I need to focus, Rhiannon. I've never done this before and I want to make sure it goes as smoothly as possible." She said.

Rhiannon nodded, but opened her mouth to speak, hopeful eyes beseeching Grandma for one more question. Deirdre smiled expectantly.

"Will it hurt?" Rhiannon asked, feeling silly.

"I certainly hope not." Deirdre replied.

By the time they had the candles set in place the sun had mostly set and the light in Rhiannon's bedroom was flickering orange. Bizarre shadows stretched across the floors and walls. They seemed to dance and sway. Rhiannon was certain that it was only the candle light, yet it was certainly spooky. Rhiannon sat on the bed, stiff and straight with the squared shoulders of someone who was being brave out of stubbornness. Deirdre had not moved from the floor. Martin stood by the door, cradling their old violin in his hands. He would come no closer than this. The fact that he was staying in the room was a testament to what these girls meant to him.

The room was silent except for the sound of Deirdre's heavy breathing. She laid her hands palm up on her knees. She was as ready as she was ever going to be. She opened her mind.

Her friends were all around her. They crammed into the room to be close to her. It was not often that Deirdre specifically came to speak to them and they felt giddy at the occasion. So often their time with her was stolen, found in the corners of her day. They did not mind because the edges of things were all they knew, but here was their Lady, making time for them. The shell fey came through the crack under the door, out from the dresser drawers, up through the floor. They squished and stretched their bodies to fit closer to Deirdre. They had come just for her.

Deirdre felt like she was in a bath of ice. Her skin stung from the weight of all the fey coming close, drawing near her and breathing in her warmth. She focused on the furnace inside her heart, stoking the fire that she knew burned there. She had to imagine that every breath was like a pump on the billows, giving life to the fire. That was the only way that she could stay here with her pets and give them the warmth they craved from her. There were so many, though. She felt the time that she'd lived through. It was so easy to do this when she was a girl. A lack of practice had left her rusty, she decided. She refused to blame it on the years.

With the eyes of a fey, Martin could see the magic that Deirdre was churning out. It bloomed, flowered and burst from her body in explosions of light. His grip on the violin tightened. The shell fey were feeding, drinking in Deirdre's heart magic like little gluttons. He hoped that she knew what she was doing.

"Friends," Deirdre said finally when she felt like she could wait no longer. She spoke softly so that her voice wouldn't shake. "I have called you here to ask something of you."

The shell fey were thrilled. They gibbered and chirped like infants. Anything for their Lady, of course! So often they had to listen for her wishes in snatches of dreams. A direct request was a welcome chance to use their powers for her.

"The child… the woman before us." Deirdre said, smiling as she corrected herself. "She is my granddaughter. You have protected her for me, as I wanted. But I have a new request."

Martin's nerves were as taut as the violin strings. This was it.

Deirdre continued. "My friends, allow her to be her own. She has strength. She will protect herself. Free her heart. I ask that you leave her, remove yourselves from her spirit. She does not need your protection anymore. Let her be her own woman."

The shell fey went still. The bow to the violin was suddenly in Martin's hands, held by his side but ready if the need arose...

The three pairs of eyes in the room snapped to the corner near Rhiannon's bookshelf. The sound was like wind in rushes, a high but hollow pulling sound. A single shell fey was inhaling, mouth opened as wide as it could. Its neighbors tilted back their head, joining in the breath, adding to the noise. Swiftly the sound rippled out, until it filled the space, so loud that it felt like it was pulling the walls slightly inward. The crowd of fey pulled the air in, so deep and full that the trinkets on Rhiannon's bookshelves trembled, threatening to topple over. Martin tried to pull the violin to his chin but Deirdre shot a hand out to him.

"Don't!" She yelped.

The magic flowing off her snapped and cracked in thin, forking tongues. The two adults looked to Rhiannon. She was breathing hard, eyes so wide that they made the rest of her look smaller. Her mouth was slightly open, as though she were trying to speak.

"I feel it. . . " She managed, then her body arched. She fell on the bed, gasping and writhing.

Martin saw it. A tiny pinprick of darkness appeared above Rhiannon's body. It ballooned out into a hole, stretching over Rhiannon's body in the blink of an eye. Faster than should've been possible, he flung aside the violin and leapt across the room, clutching Rhiannon's arm just as the girl and the hole winked out of existence, taking Martin with them.

The sound in the room stopped immediately.

The shell fey fled from Deirdre, moving in a fearful swarm away from the sudden cold. The old woman sat alone on the floor of her granddaughter's bedroom, staring at the empty space. In the quiet, she felt as though her heart had been ripped out.

. . .

Martin felt like he was being sucked up through a straw, stretched thin and rushed nauseatingly into the dark unknown. His fist was a vice around Rhiannon's forearm and he knew that if he lost his grip there was no telling where he would end up. Wherever she went, he had to be with her when they landed. If his face had peeled off by the time they landed, well, then he'd have to just grow a new one, then, wouldn't he? The strain was such that he couldn't laugh, much less smile at the dark humor keeping him sane through the horrific experience. He just had to hold on a few more seconds. At least, he hoped.

With a squelching noise, the pair arrived. Their momentum carried them through the air, flying a few feet before tumbling. Martin attempted to pull Rhiannon to him and block the brunt of the fall but it was all he could do to hold on at this point. Finally, they stopped. Martin lay on the ground, spluttering. Rhiannon lay beside him, not a scrape on her. She seemed to be sleeping in peaceful repose.

If there had been any doubt what she was before, this settled his suspicions about her with a sort of bitter jealousy. Martin hated traveling between worlds without a gate. He would be covered in bruises for a week. Druids, on the other hand, just popped back and forth without so much as a wink. Of course, most of the time they did it on purpose and with the benefit of training. He had never heard of any human spontaneously jumping between worlds right off the bat. It was impossible, and if he'd known it wasn't then there was no way he would've had her open up her magic like this. He groaned as he tried to roll over. This was well beyond his worst-case scenario predictions.

Of course, he'd never heard of shell fey creating a block in someone's magic before, either. This was new territory all around. Not to mention that it was an O'Farrell. It should not surprise him that she was a game changer. It seemed to run in the family.

In spite of the way his bones felt a bit like pudding, Martin stumbled up and tried to quickly get his bearings. He swung his head back and forth on his shoulders, wincing at the orchestra of pops and cracks. There was no time to grumble. Martin could tell by the feel of the air and the smell on the wind where they were now, and it meant nothing but trouble. She had taken them to The Otherworld, home of the fairies.

While there was always a chance that they were perfectly safe, the chance was embarrassingly slim. In fact, his old colleagues would probably have a whole host of mixed feelings at his return. They'd mentioned before that things tended to run smoother without him, although to Martin's view that just meant they were running in the wrong direction. It wasn't the best way to make friends, and here even friends were not always to be trusted. Martin found himself eager to find safety. Where, exactly, were they?

Trees drenched in thick green growth surrounded them. He could see that their roll had been stopped by thick tree roots coming out of the ground, forming a nest padded with moss and underbrush. All around them like a vivid, green ocean, the plant life rolled. It was difficult to see too much for all the trees and bush. There were a few places he knew of that had jungles like this. He needed more of a clue.

Then he saw the fruit, the green orbs hanging heavy on the trees. There were some hanging close enough that he could grab them on tip-toe, and when he pulled them down he recognized them imme-diately. That narrowed it down to one option. They were somewhere in Naga territories. He grinned, then frowned, then winced at the pain

in his spine. Perhaps he could work with this, he thought, looking

down at Rhiannon

Last time he had seen them had been exciting enough, but the

balance had surely shifted with Rhiannon's presence here. They had

the same goals as Martin, just different ideas about how to get there.

At the very least, he could allow him to feel a little bit of hope. There

were plenty of places that they could've ended up that would've been

much trickier to survive than this one.

He knelt by Rhiannon and checked to make sure she was ac-

tually breathing. Her lungs lifted and fell steadily. "Rhiannon..." He

said, gently. There was no movement. "Rhi!" He hissed, tapping her

on the shoulder.

She flinched in her sleep, and Martin recoiled as a tongue of

light flared off of her. It darted and snapped after him, but fizzed out

of existence in an instant. His heart thumped in his chest. That was

unexpected.

Martin pushed his hands through his curls, thinking. He didn't

dare shout to try and wake her. Even if he could convince the Naga to

be friendly enough, there were plenty of fey in this neck of the woods

that wouldn't be so conversational before attacking. If the same mag-

ic that ripped them through to the Otherworld was still racing through

Rhiannon, then shaking her awake was not an option. He did not want to know what would happen if this colossal, untamed power found him a threat. Touching her was dangerous in and of itself. It was time to rely on his wits, bless him.

It was so much easier to operate in the void. The place called Earth had so much of his magic around that he could do almost anything there! Here, he had yet to find a thread of music floating around. Still, there were other options for a fairy willing to take a chance. The fey of this world could cast circles around Martin at every turn, it was true, but Martin had a few tricks that they had forgotten. Let's see if he could still remember how to do them.

He slowed his breathing and held his hands out, letting his fingers flow through the air. If he let his eyes relax and go out of focus, he could see the way it bent the light around him. Wild magic. Thread. It was everywhere, so different from Earth where the strands of power were thin and frayed, play things for the broken fey that lived there. This stuff was the real stuff, rich and biting. Rich thick strands in every possible color flowed through the air, and when it felt him reaching out, it began to circle. He could feel them hunting for a vessel. Martin had to be careful. There was power here that would consume him in an instant if he let it in.

His fingers floated and danced around the thread, avoiding hungry bands of magic that tried to dive into his palm without permission. He waited, hoping beyond hope that things had not changed so much since he was last here. It had been a long time, but this was absurd. He'd never seen so much violence in the thread. How much rage had the wild magic taken in? It felt like he'd jumped into a swarm of hungry sharks with a bleeding hand. He was having to jerk and sway to keep them away.

Then, he saw it. Something soft and curious. He dipped back and very carefully extended a finger towards it, an invitation. Peacefully, it swam into his palm and gently flowed into his spirit, lighting him up. It felt like fizz tickling along his bones. His mouth felt dry and slightly sharp, like a lemon seltzer.

He opened his eyes, and opened his palm, letting the magic flow back out in the same breath that it had come to him. He'd given it his request, but these things were tricky. There was no way to be sure what the thread was even capable of. Hopefully it would find a way to grant his request.

He saw the light stream out of his palm in several threads, much brighter and clearer now than they had been before they'd come through Martin. They wiggled and wove together, dancing through the air towards Rhiannon as a net. They became more solid. It looked like a rope swing of some sort. The newly weaved hammock slid beneath the sleeping girl, even this gentle touch causing sparks of angry orange light to hiss off of her, but the net was unharmed. Martin grinned. This was perfect. The net lifted the girl into the air, hovering a few feet off the ground. Nestled in the floating bed, Rhiannon's magic seemed content to flutter close to the girl's skin.

Slowly, he began to make his way through the jungle, the hammock floating a few feet behind him. Life was harder in the Otherworld, no doubt, but he could survive. He whistled to himself as he walked. The Naga camp should be this way. Time to see if his old acquaintances were feeling friendly today.

Chapter Four

In the Otherworld

She was at Grandma's house, and yet it wasn't Grandma's house. It looked more like the inside of some church she had been to once when she was young, although she couldn't say when, but Grandma and Bear and Colin were all there. Jenny was in the house, but Rhiannon wasn't sure where. That upset her. It was important that she find Jenny.

Colin was happy to see her, though, and didn't want her to leave again. Rhiannon felt guilty when she looked at him. He looked much older than she remembered, older than Rhiannon was now.

Grandma brought her a big ,orange cat, furry and purring. Rhiannon recognized it as the cat they'd had when she was very young. Its eyes were so familiar that it hurt her heart. They were blue, the same as everyone else in their family.

"Turns out she wasn't dead after all, just lost! Funny what turns up when you go looking," Grandma Deedee said happily, thrusting the cat into her arms. The cat was heavy and warm. It was so big that Rhiannon couldn't hold it properly. She had to sit down. The cat was huge, crushing her chest, so big it was smothering her. She couldn't breathe.

Rhiannon's eyes yanked opened, her lungs jerking air into

her chest. Had she stopped breathing in her sleep? She coughed and gagged. She had to get this breathing thing under control. This was becoming a habit.

It took her a moment to realize that she didn't know where she was. The room was dark and she was lying in a hammock. Her skin was wet with sweat, her t-shirt soaked through. The blurry fog of confusion around her was punctuated with pinpricks of strange, tingling jabs through her whole body. She felt different muscles spasm under her skin. She closed her eyes again, focusing on breathing. Her throat was dry and itched with every inhale, but she couldn't swallow. It felt like trying to choke down sawdust. What had happened to her?

There were sounds coming from outside the room. People were working, shouting to one another, although it was mostly too muddled to make out. She tried to ignore it. Her head hurt too much to deal with anything at the moment.

Apparently, a quiet moment to order her thoughts wasn't an option. A voice clearer than the rest carried through the darkness, saying "She's awake."

"Please, let me see her first," said a familiar voice. Martin? Rhiannon managed to turn her head towards the sound, but the room was pitch black and the sound was still muffled. Wherever Martin was, he wasn't in the room with her. "Don't startled her, please!" he pressed. "Mitali, wait!"

A sudden crack of light on the wall widened to an open door, blinding Rhiannon. She jerked back from the glare, turning her spot-filled eyes away from the light. "I prefer it when you call me Tali." The stranger's voice said, far too loud and close for Rhiannon's comfort. "And she has to learn sometime, Gilly Martin. May as well be a friendly monster she meets first, yes? Rise and shine, pup. Your new life has begun." Whoever it was had all the prim authority of a school teacher and none of the warmth. They spoke with an accent, but it wasn't like anything Rhiannon had heard.

She heard the door close and saw the color of light shift behind her eyelids, not the blinding white of daylight, but a softer orange like firelight. Rhiannon dared to turn her head back and carefully open her eyes.

At the door was Martin, but standing beside him was a creature that baffled her. It had the body of a snake, covered completely in scales, but the torso and arms of a human. The scales came up their back and framed their angular face. It was slightly bigger than Martin, and he was tall by anyone's standards. The creature was beautiful, though, slender and lithe. Rhiannon immediately imagined a small, sleek weapon designed to pierce between ribs and find gaps in your defense, like a fencing foil or an arrow. The scales and skin of the creature were both vividly green. Rhiannon swallowed in spite of herself and hoped that her face looked braver than she felt. The way it smiled at her made her skin crawl.

"Well?" it asked. "You're awfully quiet."

"Mitali, please don't." Martin sounded desperate. "She doesn't understand! I haven't had a chance to explain anything."

"Stop talking, fox," Mitali responded, flicking her eyes to him for only a moment before looking back at Rhiannon. "So, pup? What do you have to say for yourself?"

Rhiannon winced at how sharp and loud her voice was. It was too much, and frankly she could not trust the evidence of her eyes. Perhaps this was another episode like before? She could be imagining this. She could wake up back in the living room with Jenny and Colin.

"I assure you, little one, I am all too real," Rhiannon looked up in surprise as the creature replied to her unspoken thoughts. "And you are in some terrible trouble."

Rhiannon was not sure if the creature was speaking to her or Martin, and the snake's grin seemed to deepen. "Frankly, both of you," it said, glaring at Martin as well.

"Stop, Mitali. Let her actually speak. I hate it when you do that." Martin complained petulantly, crossing his arms.

"And I hate it when you bring doom upon my people, so I suppose we'll call it even for today, shall we?" she snapped back, the tip her long green tail flicking.

"What's going on?" Rhiannon croaked, working her dry

tongue in her mouth. "Can I have—"

Before she could finish her sentence, Mitali reached out with her free hand and tossed Rhiannon a waterskin that looked right out of a renaissance festival costume. It landed heavily on her chest, making her cough. Once she started, she couldn't stop.

"Mitali!" Martin barked, sounding surprisingly like Deirdre. He crossed the room and carefully lifted the canteen off of her, but as she coughed, Rhiannon noticed he was careful not to touch her. "She's just a child!"

"Your story holds true for now, fox." Mitali snapped, unremorseful. She set the lantern on an upturned crate, the flame inside wavering anxiously with the force of the gesture. "The Speaker's decision stands. For now, tend to your young. I will be guarding the door."

"That's really not necessary-" Martin tried tiredly, but couldn't finish his words before she slammed the door of the hut.

The sounds outside the small room continued, but it was silent inside. Rhiannon looked at Martin, waiting for an explanation. He managed to shrug. "Old friend?" He offered.

"Martin, what's going on?" she croaked, trying to push herself up but unaccustomed to being in a hammock. How did these stupid things work anyway?

"Slow down! Here." Martin urged, quickly opening the

waterskin and offering it to her. Rhiannon relaxed and eagerly took the water, slurping it down. The instant relief to her throat was wonderful. She could feel it flowing into her body, all the way down into her stomach which gurgled greedily. The bag was empty too quickly.

"Any more?" Rhiannon asked hopefully, but Martin shook his head.

"Not yet. I know you're thirsty, but we have to take it slow." He sounded apologetic, which was little comfort. Rhiannon felt like she could talk now, at least.

"So can you explain things now?" Rhiannon tried again. The hammock was actually fairly comfortable, if she could just let herself relax into it.

Martin began to pace the tiny room, a funny sight considering he had less than six feet of space to work with. Finally, he grabbed an empty crate, turned it upside-down, and sat, looking squarely at Rhiannon. "Rhiannon. What's the last thing you actually remember?" He asked.

"Being in my room. Grandma was talking about me being my own person. There was a weird noise and then. . . " Rhiannon blinked, things getting fuzzy. "Something happened. Something that felt really. . . weird."

"Weird?" Martin said, "Weird, but not bad?"

"No, not really." Rhiannon said, puzzled. "Why? Was it

supposed to be bad?"

Martin shrugged. "How should I know? But feelings count for a lot. If it didn't feel bad, then it probably wasn't."

"Um. Okay." Rhiannon said, not following. "How did we end up here?"

Martin rolled his lips together to a thin line, looked at her for a moment, and then shook his head, immediately pacing again.

"Martin!" Rhiannon wished that she could move just so she could throttle him. "Why is this so difficult?"

"Rhiannon, I am currently stuck between forces of impossible weight pulling in several different simultaneous directions at once!" Martin yammered as he paced. His hands flew as he talked. "I have promises I must keep to multiple people, some of which are contradictory. I must keep you safe. I must not tell you certain things. I must be sure that you know enough not to get yourself killed! I must keep- "

"What?" Rhiannon interrupted, suddenly alert. "Get myself killed? Martin, what is this place? Why is that even a possibility?"

"Augh!" Martin wailed, burying his hands in his curls. "Rhiannon, just. . . please just give me a moment. Please!" he begged.

Rhiannon stopped talking and watched Martin mutter to himself, seeming to fluctuate freely between humming nonsense notes and strings of words that Rhiannon recognized but did not understand in context. He seemed to be sorting invisible objects with his hands, weighing them on imaginary scales. Finally, he stepped back and looked from one side of the room to the other. He took a deep breath and nodded. "Okay. I think I've got it."

"So?" Rhiannon was impatient.

"First, the rules," Martin said, holding up both hands. "I will tell you my best guess as to how we ended up here, and where here is. I will tell you the things we have to do when you leave this room. I will tell you when I can't answer a question. You may ask whatever you like, of course, but recognize that there will be gaps in the story. There are secrets I cannot tell, even if I wanted to."

Rhiannon played these words back to herself. The secrets thing bothered her, made her feel small and out of control, but she at least appreciated that he was telling her there were things that he wouldn't be telling her. "Fine," she said, and nodded her head for him to continue.

Martin clapped his hands together and sat back on the crate. He took a deep breath, and began.

"When your magic woke up, it was powerful," he said. A shiver ran through Rhiannon's whole body. "We had no way of knowing, but even my most extreme concerns did not account for this. Your power was so strong, so deep, that it ripped you through to another world. This world."

"Another world?" Rhiannon echoed, dazed.

"The Otherworld, actually," Martin continued. "I can only imagine that the sudden expulsion of magic opened a rift. It shouldn't have been possible. Druids can only do magic like that after years of training and practice. If I had thought for an instant that this could've happened. . ."

"Druid? What do you mean, Druid?" Rhiannon said. Her brain snagged on the word like a lump in her throat that would not go down.

Martin suddenly paused for a moment, staring upwards as if checking something, then nodded. "Druid is our word for creatures from Earth. That's what you've become now."

"No, Druids are like, mystical forest people from England." Rhiannon said, furrowing her brow. "That's not right."

"It's hard to explain! Is that really what you want to focus on right now?" Martin said impatiently. "I haven't even gotten to the good part yet."

"Fine," Rhiannon said, struggling to keep up. "Go on."

"The Otherworld is home to unique creatures." Martin managed, obviously struggling for a moment.

"So, you're one of them? A unique creature? Like that snake?" Rhiannon found she could not help interrupting.

"Mitali isn't a snake, she's a Naga." Martin corrected. "And, yes and no. I'm both like them and. . . my own special sort of thing."

"But not human," Rhiannon added, staring at him.

A grin broke bright and bold on his face. He winked rakishly, but simply said, "Moving on, then? I've covered how we arrived and where we arrived, but we've yet to discuss what happens next."

It felt like riding the Gravitron at the state fair, spinning so quickly that the world turned into a wild blur but with the odd sensation of being held still by the force. Rhiannon just had to ride it out and try not to hurl. "Alright. How do we get back home?"

"Unfortunately, getting back to Earth is not the first step. The first step is getting out this door." Martin said, gesturing grandly at the crude wooden frame behind him.

"Explain." Rhiannon sighed.

"Remember our word for the day? Druid?" Martin chattered. "Well, fun fact! Druids are completely banned from this world."

"And what exactly does that mean for me?" Rhiannon pressed the heels of her hands into her eyes, wanting the pounding in her head to go away. She wanted to hear what Martin had to say, but she was getting a tight, sharp pain right behind her forehead that she was certain he was contributing to.

"It means, my sweet, that there are many fey here who will try to kill you on sight," Martin said, so matter-of-factly that it took Rhiannon a second to process. She sat up, managing the swaying hammock well enough.

"Martin, you can't be serious! It's not my fault I'm here and I want to leave! What is going on? I never did anything to anyone here and they're going to kill me?" Rhiannon's voice grew louder and louder with each sentence.

"Shhh, Rhiannon!" Martin begged, coming to the hammock side and reaching for her, but he flinched back abruptly. "Youch!" He yelped, flapping his hands wildly.

"What?" Rhiannon said, shocked out of her fear. "What happened?"

Martin sucked on his finger, scowling at her. "That's another thing. Control yourself! It's one thing to be an emotional, pubescent teen and another altogether to throw magic into the mix. If you're going to be a brat, you're going to have to learn to be a calm brat."

"What are you talking about?" Rhiannon was indignant. "I didn't do anything to you!"

"Ah, you see, that's just it. You did," Martin said, holding up his hand and showing her the angry red marks already blistering on his fingers. "Don't worry, I'm a fast healer. But your magic is out of control, which makes self-control the only safeguard we have right now."

Rhiannon flopped back into the hammock, covering her face with her hands. She hated the feeling churning up her stomach. She knew that Martin said right, even if her brain rejected the words. It wasn't something she could've explained to herself even yesterday, but right now it was like fire and lightening was pumping through her blood. The only word for it was magic, she knew. It was like she'd grown a new arm. No, really it was like she discovered a third arm that she'd always had but had somehow ignored her whole life and now that she'd realized it was there, suddenly it was flailing all over the place smashing things. What was she supposed to do?

"Rhiannon, breathe." Martin had come close to her hammock and his voice was gentle beside her.

"Breathing is hard!" Rhiannon said behind her hands, refusing to look at him. She could almost feel him smile at her.

"I know, but try. Focus on the feeling of your body, your flesh. It's alright to go slowly. Go in counts of four. . . In four, hold four, out four, hold four, then in again for four."

Rhiannon didn't want to try, but she wanted this feeling to stop. Everything ached. Her head was throbbing. She felt like if she sneezed, sparks would shoot out of her nose. She sucked in a breath through her mouth and let it out in a gush.

"Good, but count. Clear your mind of anything else. Just breathe." Martin said.

Fine, Rhiannon thought, strangling the bitterness that flared up in protest. She counted.

In. . . 2. . . 3. . . 4. . .

Hold. . . 2. . . 3. . . 4. . .

Out. . . 2. . . 3. . . 4. . .

It was working. The small aches and spasms in her body uncoiled as she continued to breathe. The storm inside her quieted. It was like smoothing the wrinkles in a cloth, pushing an iron over them gently until everything felt calm and peaceful. As Rhiannon relaxed, she found her body begging to sleep. Rhiannon didn't want to sleep. There was too much she didn't know. She opened her eyes and looked at Martin. "Will you tell me more?" she asked, the tail of her sentence swallowed in a yawn.

"Yes," Martin answered, "but that can wait. If you need to sleep, you should."

Rhiannon's eyes gratefully closed, immediately drifting off.

Martin brushed the hair off of her forehead, impressed with the child. He had not expected her to be able to control it so quickly. With so much power and so little practice, he had expected it to take at least a few days before she was safe for others to be around, but almost immediately she had reined in her power. It was enough to get his hopes up.

He took the lantern and withdrew from the shed where the Naga had agreed to store Rhiannon, closing the door quietly behind him. He knew that he should be thankful for even this allowance, but he still found himself disquieted by the accommodations. Sure, he had been worried about how safe a freshly-awakened Druid would be in The Otherworld, but a storage shed? It seemed meager.

"Well, we could just leave her in the jungle for the Fenrir to devour," came a sour voice from behind him.

Martin turned to see Mitali sulking by the hut, glowering at him. He forced a smile at her and thought a few rude words in her direction. Mitali's own tight smile went tighter.

"Same to you," she said. "Gilly, we need to talk about this."

"What about it?" Martin said, turning and walking away from the shed. He knew that he wouldn't avoid a conversation with Mitali, but he wanted to be sure that Rhiannon didn't hear a word of it. Even in her sleep, it was dangerous for her to learn certain truths. Dreams could be powerful things.

"The Druid? You've thrown the balance off yet again by bringing her here. If the High Council learns of her, they will call the fey to cities in droves! They will hunt her to the ends of the world. Everything will fall apart. The Speaker is doing his best to keep things in order, but you are making it increasingly difficult for us to hold up our end of the bargain."

"Remind me again how that goes? Your end of the bargain?" Martin asked, throwing a look over his shoulder that suggested he remembered full well. "Because the last time we crossed paths you were attempting to kill me. I have yet to figure out how that factors into our arrangement."

"You were causing complete chaos!" Mitali retorted, flinging her hands up dramatically. "You wouldn't listen to reason. Clans were fleeing our side because you wouldn't shut up when you needed to. All of the fey in the pact felt you had gone too far. My Speaker was just the first to do something about it."

Martin stopped, feeling they'd gone far enough from Rhiannon, and turned on Mitali. There was no playfulness left in his gaze. "I know you are nothing but a Knife, Tali, but I always believed that you could still think for yourself," Martin snapped. "Do *you* believe that I go too far? Do you really believe I do anything that isn't absolutely necessary? Don't forget who I am, snake. I have seen things that even your ancestors have forgotten."

Mitali did not flinch. "Your relationship with the Last Druid was poisoning your judgement," she said.

Martin stared at her and gave one, cold chuckle at her words. "So, jealousy? That's what this was about? That's why you agreed to hunt me?"

In a blur, Mitali's tail slashed, striking Martin hard against the face. "You stupid fox." Mitali hissed, shaking her head. "I don't care one wit about you beyond the purpose you serve for the fey and our cause. This has nothing to do with us. You were risking too much in order to protect her. The Last Druid had to be given up and you know it."

"Don't call her that," Martin said. He'd looked down through the course of Mitali's lecture, rubbing the red mark on his face.

"What?" Mitali said, derailed.

"The Last Druid. She's not." Martin looked back up at Mitali with a grin that could start a wildfire. "She's not the last. Her daughter is here now."

Mitali breathed a sharp sigh through the slits that were her nose. "And that, Gilly Martin, is the reason why I have been told not to kill you this time around. The Druid girl needs you, clearly. But hear this. I am sworn to protect the girl, not you. If you get in her way, I will not hesitate. I am a Knife, and I know what I'm for."

"Of course," said Martin, but his smile and his thoughts betrayed his true feelings. Mitali shook her head.

"We will return the girl to the void to complete her training away from the fey. The Otherworld is too dangerous for her. You will go with her and bring her back when she is actually prepared for her task. Until she is ready, you are not to return under any circumstances. And Martin? Forget about her mother," Mitali said darkly. "I know what you think, but you're wrong. There's no way to save her. She's gone."

Martin said nothing as Mitali slithered away. "So even the mind-readers don't know everything," he muttered to himself as he watched her go. He whistled to himself he wandered back to the shed.

Rhiannon opened her eyes ready to take on the world. She had no idea how long she'd been sleeping, but it had certainly been long enough. The hammock swung gently but she managed to swing down from it with minimal struggle, only losing her balance slightly amidst the crates in the tiny, dark room. She caught herself on a shelf and accidentally knocked over some small containers that fell to the dirt floor.

The door swung upon suddenly, and Martin was there, eyes wide with alarm. Rhiannon couldn't help but chuckle at him.

"Good morning," she said with a grin.

Martin visibly relaxed and smirked back. "Evening, actually. You slept all day."

Sure enough, the outside sky was the hazy purple of twilight. "Look at that!" Rhiannon breathed, rushing past him into the world.

It was amazing. The shed was nestled on the edge of a hill, looking down into a sloping valley full of trees that looked more like towers, easily too wide for ten people to wrap their arms around. The only reason she could see the sky for all the plants was for the elevation. Even the vines growing on the outside of the small building were amazing. The flowers blooming there were the size of her face. They were striped with yellow and green, and smelled faintly spicy. Rhiannon felt like her eyes were not big enough to take in everything she saw. Then her stomach gurgled loudly. She clutched it with both hands, feeling the hunger pains. "Martin?" she asked, looking back at him.

"Ah, yes. To be expected. Come with me. We'll find something to eat," he said, placing an arm around her shoulder. "However, be aware that the Naga might be a bit apprehensive of you. After all, untrained Druids are rightly considered. . . well, unpredictable."

Rhiannon heard the words as a jab at her earlier struggles with her power. She flushed with defensive pride. "Shut up!" she snapped, jerking out from under his arm. "I'm doing the best I can, and I've only known about this stupid mess for a day. All things considered I think I'm a pretty decent Druid if I do say so myself. Nobody has anything to worry about." Rhiannon crossed her arms tightly.

"Rhiannon, breathe!" Martin said, suddenly serious.

Rhiannon wanted to round on him again, but froze when she realized the lightening was fizzing in her blood again. In frustration she stomped her foot, but she closed her eyes and counted. 1. . . 2. . . 3. . . 4. . . The buzz settled quickly, leaving her feeling tired but not nearly as exhausted as before. She hated that he was right.

When she opened her eyes, he was staring at her with concern. She was embarrassed enough that she would've stormed off from him if he wasn't leading her to food. "Carry on, please!" She jerked her head forward down the path.

Martin shook his head, lost. She went from blazing to frigid in no time at all. "Rhiannon, I didn't mean anything by it," he tried.

"Whatever. Let's just find something to eat. I'm starving." She tried her best to slouch in nonchalance as though they could pretend the outburst hadn't happened. "What do they have to eat here? I would kill for a hamburger but somehow that seems like an unlikely possibility."

Martin looked so dramatically pained that Rhiannon forgot her annoyance for a moment and nearly laughed. Fortunately, she kept it together and managed just to roll her eyes at him. "Alas! If only it were so," Martin said plaintively. "The beauty of a hamburger. It's not quite a fried egg sandwich, but I understand the craving. There are many such treasures which can only be found in your world. No, Rhiannon, I will be quite frank. The quality of food in this world is the single most disappointing element of returning to it."

"Aside from the people trying to kill me, right?" Rhiannon offered. It sounded like a joke. It was a joke, right? But her stomach turned in knots and she couldn't help but wonder. "I mean, are there people trying to kill me? Should we be worried?"

Martin shook his head. "No, no. The Naga won't let any harm come to you while you're here."

"But you said—" Rhiannon began, squinting at him, but Martin laid a hand on her shoulder and she stopped.

"Rhiannon, the Naga understand the importance of the Druids, even if the rest of the Otherworld doesn't. They will keep you safe."

As they moved through the thick underbrush, Rhiannon realized that there were Naga everywhere. The snake-people slithered through the underbrush, coiled around and up trees, hung from heavy branches high above their heads. She kept staring at them in spite of her efforts not to. They were giant but moved with smooth elegance that made them seem more fluid than solid. Most of them were brown, grey, and green, but she could spot Naga that were brilliant rainbows of color. They were stunning and terrible, like something from a movie. Her logical brain kept reject the fact that they were actually real, but there they were, close enough that if she'd dared to, she could've felt their perfectly interlocked scales. They would often look up at her and smile as she went by, but Rhiannon looked quickly away. There was something in their expressions that was not entirely friendly.

Eventually they came to a dug-out pit that was filled with fire and coals, where three Naga were working together. They all had ashy gray scales, the fire glinting off specks of orange and red in their tails. Each Naga was tending a flame and looking over slabs of rock that cradled round, green orbs in varying states of char. The heat from the pit was so much that Martin and Rhiannon stopped some ways back, squinting in the scorching air. One of the Naga came slithering up to them.

"The Speaker has said that we will feed you," they said and extended a bulging bundle to Martin.

"Thank you, friend!" Martin said cheerfully, but the creature had already turned back to their work. Martin shrugged and jerked his head at Rhiannon, indicating that they should move on.

"Who is the Speaker?" Rhiannon asked when they'd moved away from the fire pit. "That's the second time these Naga have mentioned them. Are they in charge around here?"

"Yes," Martin said. "Everyone in a clan has a job, and the Speakers make decisions for the clan. The Speaker is a part of what's called the High Council, a collection of Fey who rule the world. The Speaker represents the interests of the clan, and in turn tells the clan what the High Council has decided will happen for the world. Their word is truth."

"So they're like. . . dictators?" Rhiannon conjectured, aghast.

Martin rolled his eyes. "I don't know. That word sounds an awful lot like 'speaker' to me, but you humans tend to confuse and conflate words an awful lot."

Rhiannon took a moment to mull this over in her head as they walked, but realized it was a bigger issue than she could untangle in this moment. "Well, anyway, couldn't we ask the Speaker for help? I mean, if we got to them and explain the situation-"

"We don't need an audience with the Speaker, at least not

with the Naga. They're already getting all the information they need."

Martin interrupted, and Rhiannon knew something was wrong. His stride had lengthened, making it harder for Rhiannon to keep pace with him, and his expression was clearly preoccupied. He was acting as frustrated at Rhiannon felt, but she reasoned that in the grand scheme of things, she had it at least as bad as he did. She kept pace with him.

"Why not?" Rhiannon pressed.

"Haven't you noticed?" Martin asked, sounding venomous. "The Naga have the ability to hear thoughts, at least on some level. The Speaker doesn't need to see us face to face to tell us what they've decided. The Speaker doesn't need to use their own ears to hear what we have to say. For the Naga, one set of eyes is as good as another."

"They can read minds?" Rhiannon reached out and grabbed Martin's arm, stopping him short. "Seriously? They can read my mind right now?"

"Yes!" Martin sighed.

"Can all fey do that?" Rhiannon felt genuine panic. Could Martin read her mind? Had he been reading her mind all this time?

He gave her a sardonic look as though he had heard the worry in her mind, but then he said, "No, little love, not all fey are mind-readers. The Naga are special. It's part of the magic they were given. Each fey clan has a different vein of power."

Rhiannon relaxed a little, but shivered remembering the eyes that had watched her the whole way to the fire pit. Had each Naga dug into her brain and listened to her anxieties? That was a dreadful thought. But then another thought came to her, and she turned her gaze back to Martin. "So, what's yours?"

He seemed not to have heard her as he opened the pouch the Nagas had given him and fished out a nearly-blackened fruit. "Here. Peel off the skin first. The insides taste best," he said.

Rhiannon wanted to pry further, but the idea of filling her stomach took over and nothing else seemed to matter much. The dark skin came away easily in her hands, revealing white, pulpy fruit, steaming slightly in the chilly evening air. Rhiannon burned the roof of her mouth on the first bite, but still chewed and swallowed. She looked at Martin in confusion. "It. . . doesn't have a taste," she said, baffled. "Like, none at all."

"Yes. Now you understand."

Rhiannon took another bite and swallowed. The texture of the fruit was nice enough, squishy and juicy between her teeth. The warmth was pleasant going down her throat and into her belly as she ate. It just felt strange. She'd never put anything into her mouth that had no taste at all before.

When she'd scooped the last of the fruit out of the skin, she realized that she was no longer hungry. Perhaps not full to bursting or particularly satisfied by the meal, but she no longer wanted to eat. "Huh," she said, looking sadly at the fruit rind.

Martin finished his shortly after and pitched the rind into the nearby forest. "Go ahead. They decompose quickly," he said, gesturing to the rind she still held. Rhiannon hurled hers into the darkness and followed Martin back toward the shed, quiet and thoughtful.

"I'm not hungry but. . . somehow I still want something else," she said eventually. "Is there anything else to eat? Anything that just tastes. . . I dunno, like anything?"

"Nope," Martin said with a sigh. "The fey find it wasteful. Many of them laugh at my efforts to teach them anything about cuisine. I earned quite the reputation as an oddball after I tried to introduce them to the concept of salting food. Humans have been doing it for centuries! I don't see what's so challenging about it."

Martin looked so sad and hopeless that Rhiannon found herself pitying him. She reached out and patted him gently on the arm. "There, there, Martin. It'll be alright. We'll be back home in no time and I'll have Grandma make you some breakfast, yeah? It's your favorite, right?"

This seemed to cheer Martin up slightly, but as they neared the hut he sighed and stopped, turning a somber look to Rhiannon. "I suppose you're ready for me to tell you the plan, then?"

He stared at her for a moment. It was difficult to make out her features in the gloom, but he could see the jut of her chin, the slant of her nose. When he couldn't tell the color of her hair, he would've believed her to be Bridget. He wished deeply that he could've spent years on Earth explaining things before they'd come to this place. She was too young to be here, too old to hear these things without curiosity and hunger. He needed more time. He had even less than he was taking. In spite of himself, he reached out and placed a hand on the top of her head.

Rhiannon flinched slightly. It was a bizarre gesture, awkward and sweet all at once. It reminded her immediately of Bear and how he'd try to show he cared without having to use words. Rhiannon was stuck with a sharp pain of homesickness and resisted the urge to jerk back from Martin.

"Rhiannon," he said finally, "I know this is a lot. You're doing well to keep up this far. I'm asking you to trust me a great deal. Are you alright so far?"

Rhiannon screwed her mouth up to the side as she thought. He was her weirdo music teacher. He was Grandma's friend whom she had allowed into their home. He was from this impossible, amazing, awful world, and as far as she could tell he was trying to help her. Rhiannon's stomach seized as she realized that this man was her only connection back to where she had come from. Even if she hated to admit it, she needed him. If she started second guessing him now, there would be nothing at all to count on. She gave one stiff nod, and Martin ruffled her hair gently.

"Good," Martin said, turning abruptly and walking back into their shed. He relit the lantern as he spoke, casting dramatic shadows over the room. "Rhiannon, there is a gate that connects the Otherworld to Earth. It's hard to get to and well hidden, but it exists. The good news is that I know where it is and can absolutely get you there."

"Okay." Rhiannon said.

"The bad news is that the nearest gate is located in a place called Hub." Martin said, clapping his hands together to punctuate this word. "This is a problem. The High Council decided to make places like Hub so that fey could join together and work for the common good, which sounds wonderful in theory but causes any number of problems in practice. The place is swarming with fey of all kinds. It will be next to impossible to move freely through Hub without being caught, which you already know is not really an option."

"So. . . what's a different option?" Rhiannon said, shaking her head. "Can't I just portal us back? I got us here, didn't I?"

"You brought us here on a fluke. You're a quick learner, quicker than I've ever seen, but no Druid can make a stable gate without proper training." Martin said firmly.

"But I did, didn't I? Maybe I could just try. What's the worst—"

"Absolutely not." Martin barked, suddenly barring his teeth.

Rhiannon froze. The glint in his eye was dangerous. At her expression of fear, Martin quickly recoiled and held up his hands. "I'm sorry. I am sorry. But Rhiannon, just because you are a natural does not mean that it is safe for you to meddle with things beyond your power. Magic is not a plaything. It will devour you. Do you understand?"

No, Rhiannon thought, but she nodded anyway. Apparently, she was not convincing enough. Martin sighed, running his hand through his curls.

"Alright. . . I can't explain more right now. I haven't figured that out yet. But Rhiannon, I need you to refrain from magic until you've figured out how to not get yourself killed with it." Martin was trying to speak slowly and calmly, knowing that the weight of the situation was lost on her.

"Fine!" Rhiannon said, rolling her eyes and retreating in on herself. Martin felt the frustration bubbling in his stomach. This child! Every time he thought he was making some headway with befriending Rhiannon she lashed out in a new, unexpected form of aggression. Was it normal for children to be so unruly when they got this tall? Martin knew it had been a stressful, to say the least, but all the same, it was stressful for him as well. It seemed obvious that Rhiannon had no sympathy for this fact. He found it amazing the Deirdre had struggled through all these years without tossing the child into a volcano out of simple exhaustion.

"Right. . . Well. The point is that soon we're going to have to do this more or less on our own in a world full of beings that are rather set on destroying you," Martin continued, perhaps with more of a cheerful edge in his voice than was necessary.

"Why is that, anyway?" Rhiannon asked, looking up from her pout with a quizzical brow. Martin wasn't entirely sure he didn't prefer the sulking to the constant prying.

"It's. . . complicated." Martin managed, pinching the bridge of his nose. His head hurt from trying to think in summersaults all evening.

"No, it's not," came a voice from the door. Martin and Rhiannon turned to se Mitali standing there, arms folded. She slithered into the cramped space, taking up the remaining room. "Rhiannon, the fey of this world fear you because creatures from the void have a strange connection with our magic. You are like a sponge. The longer you stay here, the more powerful you become, until eventually you will be strong enough to defeat all of our armies singlehandedly. It is a frightening thing."

"Mitali!" Martin groaned, throwing his hands in the air. "Beautiful! Artfully done! Thank you for all of the thoughtful and well considered information you just casually threw out there. Was that absolutely necessary, snake?"

"Yes!" Mitali snapped, glaring at him. "You are slippery and deceptive! For one sworn to the truth, you manage to create all sorts of falsehoods. There is no time for this, Martin. We have to leave to-night and I will not have the Druid confused about what is at stake."

"What do you mean, from the void? And armies?" Rhiannon interrupted, raising her voice to be heard over Martin and Mitali's bickering. "I don't want that kind of power. I don't want. . . any of this. The only reason I even agreed to this is because I wanted my normal life! I want to go home!"

Mitali's reptilian eyes studied Rhiannon's face, then shrugged. "If that is your wish, so be it. Regardless, our next step is the same. We must leave this place tonight and get you safely to the fey gate."

"What's this 'we' business you keep going on about?" Martin insisted.

"The Speaker has assigned me to protect the Druid, haven't they?" Mitali retorted. "You really think that you can make it through our jungles without a proper escort? You will be slightly safer at night but you still have no chance of survival without a Knife at your side."

"Are you really a suitable guide, though, Mitali?" Martin drawled, glaring at her. "After all, last I heard you couldn't even catch a pesky fox."

Tali's scales seemed to bristle and shudder down her whole body, something Rhiannon had never seen a real snake do but was both impressed and intimidated by. "If a fox throws itself to its death, why follow? You were no longer a threat."

"Oh, of course not! And obviously, you can see for yourself, sweet pet, that I am, in fact, as dead as they come." Rhiannon tried not to flinch as Martin reached out and tapped the snub of Mitali's noes with one finger. Fast as lightening Mitali opened her jaw impossibly wide and snapped her fangs. Martin only just snatched his finger out of the way. Still, his cheeky grin persisted. "Now, now, sweet pet. None of that."

"If you would like to keep your fingers attached to your hand, I suggest you start taking this seriously," Mitali snarled. In spite of the fact that Rhiannon had thought the exact same thing about Martin in the past, she found herself feeling defensive. Who was this snake lady to threaten her music teacher?

Mitali's eyes snapped to Rhiannon, making the girl go rigid. The snake's tail twitched but she took a deep breath and smiled back at Martin. "This will be a fun journey, I'm sure. Apparently, your new little Druid wants to keep you as a pet! But both of you should remember this. I am a Knife and my oath is to protect the life of the Druid at all costs. Please, consider the full implications of this and act accordingly."

Martin opened his mouth to retort but Mitali quickly turned away and slithered off, depriving him of the chance. "Hey!" he shouted after her.

"Prepare to leave. I'll return in an hour with supplies and we will head East towards the Hub," she called back, not quite turning her head.

"Stupid snake. . . " Muttered Martin, flexing his hands. He liked his fingers. How dare she threaten them? He shuddered slightly at the thought of traveling with her. On the plus side, Mitali was a murderous, ruthless, lightening quick killer who loved her work as a weapon and would happily go after anyone who got in their way. On the down side, see the above. It certainly changed the tone of the journey to realize she would be tagging along. . . Although he knew that he could trust her, it was only in that he knew she would do what she said. He fully believed that she would tell him before she tried to murder him.

"Martin?" Rhiannon said behind him, making him turn and confront today's reality. She looked paler than usual and Martin quickly refocused on her.

"You don't have to worry about her, Rhiannon," He said, as flippantly as he could. "Tali is one of a kind, certainly, but if she's been told to protect you then that's what she'll do. She's a Knife, after all. She doesn't have a choice, really."

"What does that mean? She has to kill people?" Rhiannon asked. Her crystal blue eyes flashed as she ducked behind her familiar defense of anger, the only way she could currently protect herself from the overwhelm threatening to creep in. "Please, just back up and explain these things to me. I know there's a lot but I need to understand."

"Alright, alright. Remember when I was talking about the Speaker and the roles? Well, her job is to be a weapon. She is there to protect, to intimidate, sometimes to kill. The world is dangerous, Rhiannon. It's good to have weapons."

Rhiannon felt uncomfortable with this. It was hard to feel certain that she wasn't going to end up on the wrong side of this weapon. Another thought occurred to her and she brightened.

"Apparently the Speaker decided we were worth helping, though, right?" Rhiannon said. "Mitali was assigned to get me to the gate, so maybe that's a sign they really are on our side?"

"No." Martin said firmly, taking a minute to look directly at Rhiannon. "The Naga are on the side of balance. As soon as the scales of the world tip too far in the other direction, they will be ready to kill all of us. Don't confuse this momentary aid as an alliance, because it's incredibly important. The Naga will tell you the same thing."

"Then why are we trusting them?" Rhiannon hissed, mortified.

"Because, Rhiannon, friends are hard to find!" Martin replied, glib in the face of such a starkly depressing reality. "If we find anyone willing to help us, even just temporarily, then we should take it. The fact that the Naga want you to live is just a reflection of how bad it's gotten."

"How bad what's gotten?" Rhiannon demanded hungrily, but Martin shook his head.

"Another time, little love. I mean Rhiannon, of course. All the same. . . " Martin said, patting her head again. "There's already so much to learn. Let's save that for another time, yes?"

So much sprawled out ahead of Rhiannon and she knew that this was only the first step. Hopefully, though, it wouldn't be long until she could put all of it behind her.

Chapter Five

When You Go Looking

Martin and Mitali argued as they walked.

"So, what do you propose, then?" Martin said, words rushing on top of each other to get at Mitali. "Strolling into Hub with a flashing sign over her head? Or perhaps hiring a band to parade her through town?"

"Glamors don't work," Mitali pushed on every word as though she could tamp Martin down with the force of them. "I've never seen anyone use them convincingly!"

"Well of course it wouldn't convince you. You can read minds. That's cheating," Martin grumbled. "For the rest of us it's a little more straightforward. If you look like a walking tree person, you're a dryad. Simple. Really, fey don't have the imagination to suspect anything else!"

"It's a waste of time! If we can't get to the gate through our own means—"

"One could argue that this is just a form of disguise?" Martin suggested.

"—then there's no point! Everything could backfire if we try to cast anything onto her. Introducing thread to a Druid of this power and lack of skill? My kind don't even bother with the thread anymore.

It's more likely to take your arm off than help you these days," Mitali snarled. "Martin, don't waste our time taking more risks than we have to!"

Rhiannon rolled her eyes as she plodded behind them. It had taken less than five minutes for the debate to take over their conversation. Rhiannon may as well have been invisible.

"I'm not saying she cast it, of course. That would be stupid," Martin asked, his tone all jeering lilt and rolled eyes.

"Thank you," Mitali said.

"But we certainly could!" Martin continued, to the Naga's disgusted frustration. "Tali, if we don't use magic, we don't stand a chance. How do you propose we get into Hub *without* a glamor, then? Cover her with mud and weeds and claim she's a swamp beast?"

"What even is a glamor?" Rhiannon interjected.

Both adults stopped talking and looked back at her, Mitali with obvious disdain. Martin at least had the decency to look embarrassed that he'd forgotten her as he tried to fill her in. "It's a way of disguising humans as fey, or fey as other fey I suppose."

"But they don't work. They're cheap tricks," Mitali said.

"You're telepathic!" Martin insisted again.

"They don't work on anyone cleverer than a boulder!" Mitali retorted. She shook her head sourly. "We are reaching the edge of our settlement. This conversation can wait. We must keep our voices down."

Surprisingly, Martin obliged and fell silent as they walked through the outskirts of the village. Before long the landscape shifted. The jungle hung dense and humid around them, and she was amazed at how loud it was. It was too dark for her to see, but noises chorused around them. She assumed most of it was birds and insects. She did not like imagining what else it could be.

"You have nothing to worry about, little one," Mitali said quietly. "There is no creature in this forest who is not afraid of me."

"Really, now?" Martin drawled. "I think there's at least one that might surprise you."

Mitali looked back and gave him a smile that showed too many teeth. "No, I don't think there is, Gilly."

Rhiannon rolled her eyes. She didn't know what was going on, but it certainly seemed like Tali and Martin had some sort of 'thing' going on. If this was a movie, the whole audience would be cheering for them to get it over with and just kiss already. Rhiannon found it infuriating. If Martin was just using this as an excuse to reconnect with some weirdo old love interest then seriously, she would be better off without him.

Mitali laughed, a bright popping noise that made the creatures in the night around them scatter in fear. Martin leapt forward, crouching protectively in front of Rhiannon before realizing that she was just laughing.

"What is the matter with you, snake?" Martin snarled.

"I'm sorry, I'm sorry!" Mitali managed, controlling her giggles. "The young one just has some... fascinating ideas. Certainly, ones that I think you would be equally amused by. Shall I share, little Rhiannon? Or would you like to?"

"Shut up!" Rhiannon blurted out, heart squeezing tight with humiliation. "Just... Drop it, okay? Can we just go, please? The quicker we get out of here the better."

"What?" Martin asked, genuinely baffled.

Rhiannon squirmed away from Martin and inched towards the front of the group, willing them to keep walking and drop the conversation. If Rhiannon had not been certain that she would blunder into a pit complete with a fanged monster that would devour her, she would've charged ahead. Mitali smiled graciously slithered on, although she still wore an impish grin.

"You know, Martin," she said, "I *do* like the way the moonlight filters through on your curls. It's quite alluring."

"What is *wrong* with you? What did I miss?" Martin said, pinning her with a vicious glare. Rhiannon felt cowed, even more so by the very pointed look that Mitali gave her.

"Nothing. Just proving a point." Mitali said. "And you're right, Rhiannon, you absolutely must stay with us. I'm not sure about the pits but there certainly are plenty of pointy teeth worth avoiding in this place."

"I don't think the girl needs any more frightening, Mitali," Martin said.

"I'm not frightened." Rhiannon said, and it was true. She was mostly curious. "What's out there?"

"Let's hope we don't find out," Martin said quickly, giving Mitali a stern look. To Rhiannon's disappointment the Naga conceded. They walked on in silence once more.

They walked for hours. Rhiannon felt exhausted and bored, her feet plodding one after another without any sense of direction or meaning. Her legs ached. She thought she'd been in shape because she could run the seven-minute mile at school, but it turns out that didn't prepare her for miles of hiking in rough terrain. The droning noise of the jungle had become grating, leaving her nerves frayed. "Martin. . ." She whined. "Can we stop please?"

"No," Mitali said before Martin could speak. He rolled his eyes and stopped walking to Rhiannon's relief. She found herself sitting immediately, even knowing that Tali would probably make her stand up again.

"Tali, she's not used to this." Martin said, "How dangerous would it be to rest for a bit?"

Mitali looked back at him and glared. "Very."

"I can set up wards. For ten minutes?" Martin asked. Mitali's tail flicked angrily.

"This goes against my advice, fox." Mitali said, but she gave Rhiannon a sympathetic look. "We can stop, but be ready to leave at a moment's notice."

Rhiannon relaxed, legs aching. Martin had certainly earned some extra friendship points for the future. She rubbed the muscles in her calves and pulled out some water to drink, slurping gleefully. When she was about to offer some to Martin, she froze. What was he doing?

He stood with his hand stretched out in front of him, his fingers twitching slightly in the air. His eyes were closed in concentration, lines forming on his forehead with the focus he was giving to his bizarre activity. He was still aside from the movements of his hands, the slight twitches and pulls of his fingers.

His arm jerked back, hand clasped around something. Rhiannon could swear she saw a pale white light flicker into his palm, and as his eyes shot open they pulsed with a faint glow. In a fluid gesture, Martin clapped his hands together, took a deep breath and blew into his palms like he was blowing a soap bubble from between them. Something ballooned out and kept expanding. Rhiannon felt a shiver run across her skin as it passed over her. The bubble continued to spread out until it had enveloped Rhiannon, Mitali and Martin inside of it. They had about fifteen feet inside the bubble, and then it faded into nothingness.

"Beautiful..." Mitali murmured. To Rhiannon's surprise, Mitali was staring after the bubble of light in awe. Martin had just done something exceptional, even for this place. She replayed the gestures she had seen in her head. Was that how magic works?

Martin's grin was as smug as ever as he came to talk to Rhiannon. "Just stay here, alright?" Martin said, kneeling beside her. "Don't go walking around. The magic won't protect you outside of the wards."

"So, you just did magic?" Rhiannon said, unable to keep the urgency out of her voice.

Martin shrugged a little. "Yes. But don't get any ideas. Remember what you promised earlier? Not getting yourself killed just yet?"

"Did I actually promise?" Rhiannon said slyly.

"Don't do that," Martin said, jabbing a finger at her warningly. "It's important, Rhiannon. No magic. Not yet. It isn't something you should try without being trained for it."

"Can you at least tell me how it works? I won't try it. I promise! I actually promise!" Martin's eyebrows furrowed at her and she hurriedly added, "But what you did looked different than what Grandma did back at home, you know? When she was just sitting there? You seemed to pull something out of the air and she… well, I don't know what she did, but it wasn't that. How was it different?"

Martin sighed, rubbing his face with both hands. She was persistent, wasn't she? The nagging worm of worry in his heart warned him that if he didn't give her something she would start experimenting in secret, and that was a recipe for doom. How much could he tell her without giving her enough information for her to try it herself? One day he would teach her properly, but she wasn't ready for wild magic yet. That would take years. For today, though, he could offer her words at least.

"Martin… be careful," Mitali said slowly, and Martin felt a shiver knowing that she was right. He hated it when she was right.

"Alright, alright. I will be," Martin grumbled. Somewhere in the back of his head, a piccolo chirped in anxiety, like a bird warning its flock of an approaching wolf. But he was caught under the scrutiny of an O'Farrell girl! There was only so much he could do. He ignored the music and focused his most serious gaze on the girl.

"So, little one, you've figured out where magic lives inside of you, yes? When you breathed before, I'm sure you felt it in a part of your body. It's different for everyone. Perhaps your hands? Your neck?"

Rhiannon's brow furrowed as she puzzled this. The feeling that she'd come to think of as her magic didn't seem to center anywhere in particular. It felt like it was coursing through her veins, if anything. Maybe it was in her blood?

"I suppose." Rhiannon said, unsure if she was willing to share this information with Martin, although she wasn't sure why. It just felt too important, too sacred, to let anyone else touch it.

"Right. Well, the magic inside of you lives strictly inside of you. That's where you'll have the most control over it. When you've trained, it will be able to reach out into the world around you and change things, but for the most part, your magic is only yours."

"But I hurt you earlier!" Rhiannon interrupted.

"No, that wasn't you hurting me. That was your magic protecting you without your control," Martin corrected patiently. Rhiannon blinked, puzzling this. She looked at her hands, imagining the lightening pulsing under the skin.

"Anyway, the magic that we have inside of us isn't the whole of the magic in the Otherworld. Here, everything has its own sort of magic. It exists around us everywhere, each bit of it tied to something that exists in this plain."

"And that's what you were using? The magic around us?" Rhiannon pressed. "How do you do that?"

"For someone who isn't going to do any magic you're certainly curious," Martin chided, arching his eyebrow. "I think that's enough for today."

Rhiannon started to protest, but then caught herself. It was odd. She was ravenously curious for information, for understanding, but she didn't know why. It wasn't like she *wanted* to do magic. The only thing she wanted was to go home and return to a normal life, to learn how to control this power so that she could hang out with Jenny without having to worry about hurting her or accidentally blowing up their house. She didn't care about this stuff. At least, she didn't want to care about it. Rhiannon felt a swelling, hot pool of shame boil in her stomach and she quickly shook her head.

"You're right," Rhiannon said, so brisk that she startled Martin. "I don't really care."

The teen turned away and started adjusting her pack.

Martin hesitated, feeling that there was something else to say but floundering in the face of this sudden emotional chill. Hopefully he glanced over at Mitali. Her own expression of concern did nothing to sooth his sour stomach. As casually as he could, he wandered over to her. She gave a meaningful look from him to Rhiannon.

"Yes, I know." Martin said, shaking his head. "I don't have to read minds to know what you're thinking."

"But Martin, if she turns her back on this place completely. . . She seems set in her heart. When she was learning the ways of magic I thought certainly we would have to keep her away from this place by force she was so hungry and curious but just there, she suddenly stopped. She withdrew completely from the subject like it was poison to her. Why?" Mitali demanded, speaking in low tones.

"She will help us," Martin insisted. "She isn't ready yet, but-"

"This is not the life she wants," Mitali insisted. "How can you be sure that she won't turn her back on our world? It would not be the first time."

"Trust me. I know what I'm doing," Martin said.

"Trusting you has caused problems in the past, fox," Mitali reminded him, but her expression was gentle, nearly concerned. It was as close to sympathy as Martin could expect from her, and it made him uncomfortable.

He shrugged. "All part of the plan, Tali."

"Hey guys?" Rhiannon said, approaching them with her pack on. "I think I'm ready now."

Martin looked at Mitali, who nodded. Rhiannon watched Martin reach out into the air again and saw the briefest flicker of light at his fingertips. She felt the air shift around her, like a tightly sealed jar had just been opened. The ward must be gone now. Mitali started off, slithering in the direction they had gone before.

Something burst from the trees, blurring between Mitali and Martin towards Rhiannon. Rhiannon shrieked. Mitali's tail shot out and latched onto the leg of a grizzled, fur covered beast, bringing it to the ground. Rhiannon had never seen anything like it. She couldn't be sure if it looked more like a dog or a bear.

"Martin!" Mitali said stiffly. Two curved blades were now in her hands. They looked so sharp that Rhiannon's insides ached just looking at them. Rhiannon realized what was going to happen and clamped her face into her hands just before Mitali plunged the blade into the creature. It whimpered. The wet sound of the sword left Rhiannon feeling ill.

"Rhiannon, don't mo-" Martin began, reaching towards her, but was interrupted by another massive gray thing colliding with him. Rhiannon leapt back, whimpering in fear at the snarling jaws and beady, almost human eyes.

Martin moved fast, kicking and squirming out of the monster's arms like a fish wriggling for freedom, but then it sunk in claws. Martin yelped, the squeak of an injured puppy, and went stiff as blood blossomed through his pant leg around the monster's claws. It growled, a guttural noise from its chest.

"Martin!" Rhiannon screamed, trembling where she stood. Some frantic part of her looked around for a rock or stick, anything she could use as a weapon. Her hands shook. It felt like the world was blurring by her. She couldn't see straight. Martin pulled at the beast's paw with his hands while trying to use his free leg and elbows to keep back the monster's open fangs.

Rhiannon didn't look away in time to miss the sight of Mitali's blade sliding elegantly through the creature's chest. The look on its face played in slow motion, a moment of surprise before screwing up with pain. It went limp and fell.

Now everything was too quiet, too still. Her hands wouldn't stop shaking. The thing was dead, and she had watched it die. Rhiannon's sick, anxious dread made a fog around her head. She had never really seen anything die before, not like this. She felt tears rolling out of her eyes although she was too stunned to do anything but stare.

Martin was still tangled in the beast's arms, wincing and whimpering as he tried to extract the claws from his thigh. Rhiannon snapped back to reality and forced herself to move forward. "Martin…" She murmured, kneeling beside him. It looked as though the claws were barbed, a cruel design obviously meant for tearing and rending flesh. Now that they were embedded in Martin, it was going to be a struggle to get them out.

Mitali lowered herself down to inspect the wound as well. "This is why we shouldn't have stopped." She said. Her tone was cool to the point of nonchalance. Rhiannon looked at her with incredulity.

"That's a rotten thing to say!" Rhiannon snapped, "Help him!"

She stared at Mitali, who did not move. Martin did not look at either of them as he struggled with the claws. "Rhiannon, please…" he begged. There was blood everywhere.

Rhiannon swallowed and reached out with shaking hands. She touched the paw of the creature and flinched back. It was still warm. Martin let loose another yelp of pain from the touch.

"Sorry! Sorry," Rhiannon said, wincing at the noise. "Oh, Martin! Just. . . just hold on. I'm sorry." She gritted her teeth tightly together and forced herself to move without thinking, trying to shut her ears to the awful sounds. The paw was heavy, but with two hands she could rip it out of Martin's leg. Martin howled. The claws took strings of flesh with it.

With his leg free, Martin seemed slightly more relaxed although his color was very wrong. He carefully pulled himself away from the beast's dead body, trying to move his injured leg as little as possible. Rhiannon tried to help. She didn't know what it the monster was, but as she shoved its bulky corpse aside, it really did seem like some sort of mix between a bear and a wolf. Her stomach lurched and she held her breath to keep the bright, stinging smell of iron out of her nose. She could not think about what she was doing or the blood that covered her now. She simply had to keep moving.

After a few minutes that felt like hours, Martin was leaning against a tree, breathing heavily and trying to inspect his wound. "How bad is it?" Rhiannon asked. Martin did not answer her. He just looked at Mitali, a question in his eyes.

"No," She said. She had stood immobile through their struggle and stared at them now with frigid gravity. "I'm sorry."

"What?" Asked Rhiannon, dread coming over her.

Martin closed his eyes and leaned back against the tree. "Rhiannon, please, this isn't something you should worry about." He said. He was using his flippant voice, the one that made her want to scream at the best of times. She wanted to shove the words back into his mouth, to make it stop. He shouldn't be talking like that right now.

"Listen, don't wait up for me," He said.

"What?" Rhiannon spat, face a mask of disbelief and frustration. "You're crazy if you think we're leaving you."

"We can't stay here." Mitali intoned in the same calm voice that made Rhiannon want to scream.

"Obviously we have to," Rhiannon snapped, glaring at Mitali. "He can't walk on that! We have to stay here until he can get up."

"Rhiannon, really, I'll catch up when I can. Just go on ahead with Mitali and—"

"No!" Rhiannon shouted. If it wasn't for the fact that he was already bleeding profusely then she would've shaken him. "No, no chance. I'll get something to make a bandage. We can clean this out. We can take care of you! We're not going to—"

"Rhiannon," Mitali said. A shiver ran down the girl's spine. There was a dark indifference in that voice, a wall that would not budge. "We must go."

But the quick burst of fear evaporated under the heat of rage Rhiannon felt. How dare she? She wheeled around to face Mitali, cold fire in her glare. Rhiannon felt like she could shoot lasers from her eyes if only she thought hard enough. She certainly hated Mitali enough to want to try. Where was her magic when she needed it?

"Listen here, snake." Rhiannon spat, poking her in the chest with her finger. "You're a Knife, right? Sworn to protect me? Well guess what? I'm not going anywhere without him. If you want to do your job, then you better figure out how to help Martin because I'm not moving from this spot without-"

Mitali's tail shot out and hit directly on the base of Rhiannon's skull. The surprise was followed by pain swimming through her head. Her eyes rolled up, flickered shut, and all she saw was a flash of white before she was out.

"Really?" Martin demanded as Mitali caught Rhiannon in the same tail that had knocked her unconscious. "That's how you protect her? Some guardian you're turning out to be, Tali." Could he walk? Did he dare to try? His leg burned cold, so much so that he wanted to find a hole to curl up in to never to move again. He felt ill and the sweat beading on his skin made him feel clammy. Still, the fear of letting Mitali slither off with Rhiannon like this was enough to make him fight back, struggling to keep himself upright.

"Your Speaker will be disappointed in you!" he tried.

"My task was to return the Druid to her world. It is your fault for bringing her now, when she knows so little that she's nothing more than another of your disasters. She refused to come with me to the gate. I had little choice. Sometimes there is a degree of damage that must be done to ensure the maximum safety of a subject." Mitali said as though reciting a pledge.

"Why doesn't that argument ever work for me?" Martin protested.

Mitali sighed, looking at Martin in his pitiful state. "I will miss you, fox. It is unlikely that you'll survive this."

"Eh, I've made it out of worse." Martin said, trying to be glib but mentally running the math and realizing she was probably right. He was tempted to just saw off the leg to get rid of the pain. Still, he forced a grin. "After all, I once outran a Naga who was out for my blood. Compared to that, surviving in these woods with one leg will be a picnic!"

"I don't know what a picnic is," Mitali said, "but goodbye, Gilly Martin."

"Mitali wait!" Martin yelled, but it was too late. With Rhiannon coiled in her tail and her swords glittering in her hands, Mitali slithered away.

. . .

Everything hurt when Rhiannon woke up, particularly her

neck and back. Her body was contorted in a constrictive knot, held by smooth, cold binds. The taste in her mouth was stale and dry. Her mouth had lolled open at some point in her unconsciousness. Working her tongue around wasn't helping. She needed something to drink. She opened her eyes in darkness and realized that she was moving. Coiled in Mitali's tail, she'd been carried off.

"Stop!" She tried to croak with her throat itching like sandpaper. Rhiannon pushed against the tail that held her, but Mitali constricted tighter and the pain in Rhiannon's back made her freeze.

"Do not struggle, little one. I will get you to safety even if you are too much of a fool to save yourself." Mitali sounded so calm. Rhiannon clinched her fists and continued to shove at her tail.

"Screw you!" Rhiannon tried to shriek, the noise coming out as a raspy hiss.

Mitali's sigh was tired and old. She kept slithering. Nothing Rhiannon did seemed to make any difference. Her nails were too short to even think about scratching through the thick scales surrounding her, and she was far too weak to actually push out of the snare she was in. Still, Rhiannon kept struggling.

"You are just going to wear yourself out, Rhiannon." Mitali said.

"Yeah, well, I'll drive you crazy in the process!" Rhiannon replied squirming so that she could arch her back and kick against the tail. "You're horrible and mean and I *hate* you!"

Mitali didn't respond but Rhiannon could practically feel her roll her eyes. She strained her vocal chords to force out another shriek, the sound horrible and resonating in the tiny chamber. She felt like she was going to explode. She had never felt this way before.

Rhiannon remembered all at once the magic and suddenly the feeling took on new life. She could use it! The sparking heat was coursing through her blood, churning around her body and looking for a way to get out. Rhiannon gritted her teeth, not knowing what she was doing, and pushed the feeling towards her hands, imagining fire shooting from her fingertips.

Nothing happened.

"What?" She whispered to herself. She tried again, pushing harder. "Come on! Come *on!*"

"Do you understand now? You don't know how to use it on purpose. It is not something in your control. This is why you need to return home a quickly as possible," Mitali was so composed that all Rhiannon wanted to do was to hurt her, to make her feel some ounce of the pain and rage Rhiannon had coursing inside of her. How dare she pretend like everything was fine? They'd left Martin to die.

"Martin is not our concern, Rhiannon. Your safety is," Mitali continued gently.

"Get out of my head!" Rhiannon shrieked, pounding the tail

with her hand. A rush of blood to her head made her suddenly woozy. She reeled, pressing her palms to her forehead. Warm pin-pricks tickled the inside of her skull, an itch she could not scratch. For the slightest moment, her fear and uncertainty bubbled up stronger than her rage. She wondered if Mitali would tell her what was going on.

But Mitali didn't say anything.

Rhiannon did know the snake well, but she had yet to have a passing thought that the Naga hadn't replied to conversationally. It was strange enough to make her wonder.

Rhiannon experimentally tried thinking, *Mitali is a disgusting snake and she and Martin are going to have lots of ugly, weird snake babies,* and braced herself for a reaction.

Nothing.

Rhiannon felt a rush of wild and eager joy. So maybe she couldn't attack with her magic in the outside world yet, but here was something! If Mitali couldn't read her mind anymore, then maybe there was a way to outthink this problem.

Rhiannon tossed her hair out of her face and tried to shift to a more comfortable tangle in her prison. It usually worked to break things down slowly, to see if there were any cracks, so she relied on simple questions. That was the best way. She could do this.

What was the problem? She had been captured by a giant snake lady and her only friend in this world was bleeding to death somewhere in this jungle. What did she need to do? Escape and save Martin. Well, first she would have to find Martin. Okay, so what did she have to use? The clothes she was wearing. Her hair. Her teeth and hands and feet. The pack she'd been wearing was gone.

None of this was any use to her right now. What she needed most of all was help. Who could help her here? Martin was out of the question. There was nobody else she knew besides the Naga, who were clearly part of the problem. There had to be another resource she could find, some tool to help her get out! What could she do to break free of Mitali's tail?

An image popped into her mind; Martin, standing under the trees' canopy, hand held out as though he were searching for something. She had seen him move, jerking back like his finger had snared something, and then there was a light. . . The magic of this world, right? It hadn't made sense but maybe, just maybe, she could copy the gestures. Magic was here, right?

In spite of herself, she flinched remembering her promise and the repeated warnings she'd been given. This was probably a very bad idea. But really, she'd already used her own magic, hadn't she? How different would it be? Anyway, from where she stood, the alternative was letting Martin die, and that meant there were no alternatives.

It was time to make a potentially horrible decision.

Rhiannon managed to wiggle so that there was a small bubble

of space inside the cocoon of Mitali's tail. "Mitali, we have to go back! Please!" Rhiannon cried for dramatic effect. She knew Mitali wouldn't turn around, but she also knew that if she got too quiet, the Naga would catch on and stop her immediately.

"That is not an option," Mitali replied stonily, slithering on.

Rhiannon had to hurry. Fear churned inside of her. If she let herself feel it, though, she wouldn't be able to do what had to be done. She could be afraid later. For now, she had to act. Rhiannon closed her eyes and unfurled her fingers, feeling for anything that seemed magical.

At first there was nothing. It was hard to concentrate, but she kept breathing like Martin had showed her in before. She tried to imagine an open bubble inside of her, a bubble that was a space for magic to come in. She found herself twitching her fingers slightly, the same way she'd seen fishermen twitch bait to lure fish. *Come on...* she thought, beginning to feel desperate. How would she even know what it felt like? Would she be able to tell the difference?

She yelped in pain. Something snagged around her pinkie. It felt like a strand of frozen spider webbing, but it dug into her, coiling around the bone of her finger. The air grew colder around her.

The tail around her whipped off so quickly that Rhiannon fell to the ground, banging her head against the rocks and dirt, but she could hardly feel it compared to what was going on inside of her. The cold, sharp pain slithering through her hand and up her arm consumed her focus.

"You mindless idiot!" Snarled Mitali, both swords pointed at the girl. Rhiannon dully watched her gestures, but Mitali seemed to be moving too slowly, her words coming from far away. "You have ruined everything!"

Rhiannon couldn't respond. The air smelled like mint and cold, a biting smell that stung her nose and throat. It had been muggy in the jungle, but she began to shiver from the inside out. Rhiannon squeezed her eyes shut. Frost coated her eyelashes immediately. She had to focus on what was going on inside of her. She could not worry about Mitali right now.

But it was already too late to worry about much of anything, wasn't it?

Rhiannon's breath caught in her throat at the thought. It had been her mind, her voice in her head, but she had not brought the thought into existence. It had come from somewhere else. The cold inside of her deepened, creeping through her stomach and into her legs. She was not sure she could move even if she wanted to. Her mouth tasted of spearmint.

You should sleep, she thought from the somewhere else place. The thought was deep in her mind, resonating through everything. *You will feel better if you let go.*

Rhiannon wanted to. If she let go and slept, if she surrendered to the cold, then she would be happy. It would be good to be a vessel, particularly to a power such as this. It was an ancient power, one that had taken hundreds before her. There was no shame to falling to the likes of it. She could feel the colossal weight of glaciers in her chest, slowing each beat of her heart. She dreamed that she had been tucked under a blanket of deafening snow, pristine and deep. It would be better to just sleep.

No. She thought, and this time the voice was her.

The thing inside of her, the ancient cold, had not expected this. Where had that come from? It had found this willing body and happily accepted the sacrifice. It had been a long time since it'd found such an easy vessel to consume. What kind of an offering refused its new denizen? The cold sank deeper, looking for the place of resistance. It had to be removed before this could be its new home.

Ah yes, there it was. It was warm, crackling bright, but it was small and easily quenched. As soon as it was gone, the vessel would surely comply.

But as soon as the creeping tendrils of cold neared the small flickering light, it was gone, suddenly somewhere else. Again, the power reached for the speck of someone else inside of its new body, and again it was gone just at the last moment. The cold rattled with anger. The power had never had such trouble extinguishing a light before. Just what was this creature? The little light vanished again and the cold dove after it. This wretched fleshling was not going to best it! Not after a life of millennia.

It stopped, not by choice. It could not move. It tried, but something was holding it back, sticking it to the spot so that it could make no more progress towards the light which was nearly in its clutches. To make matters worse, the cold could finally see that the light was not just evading it, but growing brighter. This had never happened before. It was an ancient force, born with the dawn of the world, and yet this fragile little thing defied it? It screeched with rage in its vessel's voice. *What do you think you are, creature of flesh? You are worthless, disposable, empty.*

Rhiannon was struggling. It did not feel like she was going to make it out of this, but all she knew was that she could not give up. She could still feel the difference between her and it, and she did not want to lose the part of her that was Rhiannon. She kept looking for pockets of warmth inside of her, clinging to them, breathing to fill those places up. In, hold, out, hold. She could not let the cold take over, or she would stop being herself. She would lose everything that made her real. She would cease to be.

The fear and anger at this realization made Rhiannon's fingers clench into fists, crackling through the thin frost that had formed on her skin. *I belong to myself.* Rhiannon thought, forcing all the heat she could manage into the thought. *This body is mine. It belongs to me.*

The cold raged. It burrowed into her, tunneling like a worm through her soul, so sharp and painful that Rhiannon whimpered, tears crystalizing in the corners of her eyes. Her lungs and heart protested against the sudden frigid vice around her chest.

"No!" Rhiannon forced the word out from between her blue lips, weak though it was.

She belonged to herself. She was not going to give anything to this power. She was not going to give in. She was not done fighting yet. The cold's surge faltered, just shy of extinguishing the spark. It wailed in desperation, pressing in on all sides to get at this small, flickering thing but held back by something it could not understand.

Rhiannon smiled thinly, creasing lines in the frost on her face as she realized that she could hold her ground. She was tired, so tired, but she was not going to lose. It was time to show this monster who was really in control.

You are mine! Rhiannon thought savagely, growling back at the force inside of her. *You came here, expecting a meal to consume, but I will not give in. You are a part of me now. Now you belong to me!*

Rhiannon felt her way into the spark. She put all of herself there, every ounce of stubborn pride, ever fleck of passionate joy, every memory, every dream. She fed all of her fire into the bit of her that held back against the cold and told it to blaze.

The heat rolled through her like a tidal wave, suddenly overwhelming the cold and pushing it back. Unthinking beyond fear and pain, the cold scrambled away. It tried to escape back to the world beyond, but every time it found a gap to escape this vessel, a massive wall of fire blocked its path. *What are you doing?* The denizen screeched. This was not the way things were done. Nothing like this had ever happened before! Rhiannon ignored it.

Trapped, the cold faltered, struggling to hold on to the scraps of this vessel's soul that it had claimed, letting go of the worthless body to try and keep a foothold on the creature's heart. It clung there like a cornered rat, fangs bared but waiting for death. There was nothing more it could do but sit here and wait for the end.

Rhiannon opened her eyes, panting. She was drenched in sweat and melting ice steaming off of her skin. Her stomach wanted to throw up, but her body hurt too much to even think about it. Her lips curled up into a smile in spite of herself. Bubbles of laughter came up her throat and popped in the air, unbidden. She was hysterical, she knew, but it just felt so good to still be her. It had been a terrible idea to try this, but somehow, she had come out alright.

And the cold was still there, inside of her. It belonged to her now.

End it. The thought came to her from the power. She blinked hard. Well, that would take some getting used to.

Do not just trap me here, fleshling! Destroy me or free me! That is the way of things.

Rhiannon shook her head, but thought back. *No. I need your help, so you're going to stay with me for a while. I'll free you when we've saved my friend.*

The power raged inside of her, but Rhiannon gritted her teeth and threw blazing walls of fire around the cold to quiet it. She couldn't worry about that for now.

She tried to move, shifting her weight to get her arms underneath her, and stopped. The sharp edge of a blade just kissed her throat. Rhiannon kept perfectly still, but turned her eyes to see Mitali glaring at her. The Knife looked prepared to kill her.

"Mitali, it's me…" Rhiannon said slowly. She quickly lowered the walls she'd put up in her head, opening up her mind to the Naga again. "Read my mind. You'll know. It's me."

The serpent-woman's eyes widened then narrowed as they searched the girl's face.

"This is wrong. The magic is still inside you." Mitali growled. The blade's gentle touch became the slightest pressure, not quite breaking the skin. "Send it out. Now."

"No." Rhiannon said without thinking, and winced as Mitali let her blade draw blood. It was the slightest wound but it took her back. "Mitali, it's mine now. If I let it go…"

Then it will all have been for nothing. The cold completed the thought. The magic was throbbing inside of her, restless and brooding. *But how long do you think you can hold me, creature of flesh?*

"Shut up." Rhiannon muttered.

Mitali peered at Rhiannon carefully. "I hear your thoughts, but I do not understand. There seem to be two of you now. How is this possible? What have you done?"

"I just... I trapped it." Rhiannon said, not sure at all if this was the right term. She was stuck at an uncomfortable angle, her weight on one elbow while the other hand tried to hold herself away from the blade. "Mitali, I beat it. It didn't take me over, and now it's mine. It *is* mine." She repeated, both at the snake's expression and the swell of incredulity she felt coming from the power.

"You cannot possibly hope to tame a power such as that. Wild magic is not meant to be carried in a host. I cannot allow you to continue if you don't release it." Mitali demanded, but her sword eased slightly. "I have never seen the likes of this."

"Yeah? Well me neither." Rhiannon said with a glibness that would've made Martin proud. Mitali's glare darkened. Rhiannon sighed. "Mitali, I don't need enemies right now. I need to save Martin. If you try to stop me..."

She won't be able to stop us. She knows this. The thought still felt bitter but there was a preening smugness to it now. Rhiannon smiled to herself. It was good to know that the magic was full of itself.

Us, huh? Rhiannon responded. The cold immediately started sulking again.

Mitali's serious expression cracked into a grin that made Rhiannon's stomach turn sour with dread. "I can hear you, Old One," the Naga said, "and I would not be so sure of your powers now. It would not be so hard for a Knife like me to slay you. You are mortal now, trapped in a creature of flesh. Are you really happy to be some-one's pet?"

The stab of cold in Rhiannon's chest took her off guard and she fell back on the ground, arms around her ribs. "Stop that!" Rhiannon said, both to Mitali and the power that was struggling against her again.

"This is how it will always be, stupid girl." Mitali insisted, her blades still held ready. "For as long as you hold that wild magic hostage, it will fight for control of you. Are you certain that you will always win? Are you ready for the consequences if it takes you over?"

Rhiannon vastly preferred Mitali's anger to this calm, snide lecturing. The girl glared up at Mitali. Who did she think she was? Cold pain came in throbs in her lungs, the thoughts of the magic a tangled mess with her own frustrations. Her anger at Mitali and the anger of the cold wove so closely that she could not be certain where one feeling ended and the other began. It wanted out. Mitali was the worst.

"If you can't manage to even get off the ground, how could you ever defeat me in battle? You are pathetic." Mitali continued, shaking her head in disgust. She held her swords at the ready, body coiled for a fight. Something in Rhiannon was ready to attack, but she couldn't. The cold wasn't supposed to be a weapon, just an aid. She didn't want to hurt anybody. She just wanted to save Martin.

Still, Mitali was looking at her with such superiority. She couldn't deny that she wanted to wipe the smirk off of her face. Rhiannon gritted her teeth, feeling stretched thin and achingly cold. Everything hurt. The power was still contained, but it flung itself against her constraints, radiating from her heart and seeping hurt into her blood and bones.

And Mitali was just watching her struggle in pain. She watched as though it wasn't her stupid fault they were in this mess to begin with! The stupid, wretched creature!

She should just die!

A shard of ice materialized in the air between Mitali and Rhiannon and shot towards the Naga like a bolt. Mitali's blade moved and shattered it in mid-flight. Rhiannon gaped, her anger suddenly gone. The pain from the cold disintegrated.

Had she done that?

"Yes, little one." Mitali said, her expression softening as she put away her blade. "You did. Or rather, you and your new friend did."

"I'm… I am so sorry," Rhiannon stammered, horror leaving her hollow and pale. Rhiannon had wanted to kill her. For a split second, she had wanted nothing more than to see Mitali dead, and then…

Rhiannon's face screwed up, tears welling into her eyes. She curled herself up and sobbed heavily into her knees. She had tried to kill her. Rhiannon had actually tried to kill her. She wailed, unable to contain it. Her clothes still smelled of blood.

The Naga placed a hand on her back. "It is alright, Druid. You understand now."

"But I meant it, Mitali! I really meant it." Rhiannon shook her head and tried to move away from the affectionate hand on her back. "I never wanted to hurt you. That wasn't the point! I just wanted to help Martin… I'm so sorry."

"Rhiannon." Mitali said sternly. Two strong hands pulled her up so that she was forced to look at the long, green face of the creature in front of her. "I forgive you. You needed to see this, because you needed to know. This power is strong, and it is angry. You have a temper that you cannot control, and it will use it to break free. Do you understand? If you cannot control your emotions, you will not be able to contain this power. You need to release it, little Druid. You have done well to keep it at bay, but you need to let it go."

Rhiannon heard the sincere intensity in Mitali's voice, knew that she was probably correct, and yet…

"What are we going to do?" Rhiannon asked, "Are you going to go back and help Martin?"

Mitali hesitated, but shook her head. "I do not think it is wise. Helping Gilly Martin will not expedite your return to your world. It will change too much of your path, delay your return to your family by too much."

"But we can't just leave him," Rhiannon insisted. "He promised to stay with me and help me. He followed me here to protect me! What kind of a person would I be if I turned my back on him after something like this? He would never have abandoned me. And even if he would, it's not right to leave people to die. It's just not."

"You are more important than he is." Mitali replied, obviously impatient. "He is just a fox, and you are— "

"He is my friend!" Rhiannon snapped and stopped short. Had there been a flutter of cold in her chest? Was it coming back? She took a deep breath and started again, forcing herself to remain calm. "He is my friend. I don't know what your metric of importance is, but I don't care. As far as I'm concerned, I'm not more important than anyone, and nobody is important enough to justify leaving someone else to bleed to death."

Mitali leaned back from the pup and stared at the sky, breathing deep. She understood from the girl's thoughts what was before them, but she wondered if the girl did.

"So, you are telling me," Mitali said slowly, "that you will not release this wild magic, because you do not trust me to go help Martin. You are going to keep the power, to try controlling it, in spite of the fact that it will always be waiting for the chance to consume you. You are putting yourself at extreme risk to save the life of one pitiful, worthless fey."

"Don't talk that way about him," Rhiannon retorted stiffly. "But yeah, that's the basic idea."

Mitali very slowly put her swords away, moving as though it was a real struggle to let go of her weapons. "I will protect you as best I can."

Chapter Six

Struggle

They had come, as he knew they would. The Fenrir were not creatures to waste a wounded prey. He could see five of them and hear more in the darkness. After he had stopped their first few attempts to drag him off, they had kept their distance, but it was only a matter of time before Martin's magic ran out. If only he were on Earth, these dogs wouldn't stand a chance. Alas, the hundredth time thinking the thought did not make bring it any closer to reality.

Every breath felt like syrup in Martin's lungs. He wanted to close his eyes. They flickered shut, just for a moment, and a brave, young wolf dared to lunge for him.

Groaning, he jerked up and pulled an invisible violin to his chin. His other hand dragged a bow across the strings. The splintering sound was only the memory of a note, but the wolf yelped pathetically, just a breath away from Martin's ankle. It skittered back to the others of its pack. The pack growled impatiently, pacing.

Martin glared back at them, wrestling the exhaustion inside of him back. How long could he keep this up? The good news was that his leg didn't hurt so bad anymore. The bad news was that he was having a hard time feeling anything now. When he tried to inspect his leg, he could see that it was turning a worrisome shade of purple. His magic was smoldering inside of him, doing what it could to provide him strength. Realistically, Martin knew that it wouldn't be too much longer. Then the wolves would come.

He wrapped his hand into a fist. This was not who he was. Gilly Martin did not wait for the darkness to take him, but charged forth into the shadows laughing all the way. It wasn't over until he said it was. At the very least, he wasn't going out without a show.

In a haze he shifted his hands, the left wrapped around the neck of a guitar, the right poised over the strings. As he plucked, floating notes trickled down like falling snow. He pulled out a slow, plodding rhythm underneath. Every note sent a shimmer of yellow-orange light through the ephemeral guitar. He took a breath. He sang out with pain and pleading. The air quivered with a high lonesome feeling.

"Oh, baby don't you want to go?

Oh, baby don't you want to go?

Back to the land of California,

to my sweet home Chicago. . ."

The wolves around him began to yip and whimper. One leaned back and howled. They were creatures of the hunt, of darkness. They knew of the pain of blood and bone. This ache of the soul was not their world and it burned in ways they did not understand. Martin just sang on.

"Now one and one is two,

two and two is four.

I'm heavy loaded, baby,

I'm booked, I gotta go. . .

Cryin' baby, honey, don't you wanna go?

Back to the land of California,

to my sweet home Chicago."

The music was a balm for his soul. It pulled out something that had been festering inside of him and let it float out into the world. The warbling, piercing notes seemed to make the very trees lean in. Some of the wolves began to retreat, scampering back to the safety of a wilderness they understood, but the smell of blood was still strong. It was not yet enough to drive off the whole of the pack.

Martin reveled in the feelings. The music, its power, its ability to speak on this level beyond words and beyond vision, this was what he was made of. He sang for all he was worth, knowing that this might be his last serenade. If the magic did not take him, the wolves surely would. Might as well give it his all. He leaned into the magic inside of him, shining to his fullest even as it drained his feeble body. The music in his head begged him to stop, clanging in dissonance to the song Martin was belting out, but Martin ignored it. There was no point in holding back now.

So much so that he didn't feel the cold.

He didn't hear the sound of blade slipping through flesh.

The power required to hold the guitar in place became too much, but Martin pressed on, singing alone in a raspy wail.

"Somebody will tell me

that you need my help someday,

cryin' hey. . . hey. . . Baby don't you want to go?

Back to. . . back to. . ." There were arms around him, clutching him tightly. He could hear something outside of himself. It was getting in the way of his music, the shaking of his shoulders making it hard to hold a note. He was offended at the interruption and tried to swat away the arms, but found he couldn't quite remember where his hands were.

"Martin!" Rhiannon screamed. She shoved his shoulders back and forth as hard as she could. His eyes had glazed over. He was limp. His body was so warm that it felt like Rhiannon was going to burn her hands holding him, but she squeezed tightly, ignoring the pain. "Martin, look at me!"

Mitali finished off the last wolf and came to her side. Her blades were red from the kill. She studied him carefully. "He's still in there," She said. "I can hear his thoughts, though they are distant."

"Why is he like this?" Rhiannon demanded. "What was he doing? It sounded like-"

Martin's hands floated up and cupped Rhiannon's face, freezing her in place and stopping her words. She stared at him. He stared back, blinking hard as he tried to focus. "Martin?" Rhiannon said hopefully.

His eyes cleared for a moment. He studied Rhiannon carefully, and saw what was inside of her now. He made a little *tch* of disappointment and swung a woozy head to Mitali. "I leave you with her for ten minutes and this happens?" He slurred. In spite of his obvious delusion, his eyebrow managed a perfect arch.

Rhiannon felt relief wash over her for a moment. He was still in there somewhere, even if he was clearly not okay. Her relief was short lived as he collapsed on top of her. "Martin!" She groaned, struggling under the weight of him.

Mitali was there, wrapping her strong tail around him and pulling him up into a safer position. "He is very weak now," Mitali said. "I don't know what he was thinking, pushing himself like that. You two make a perfectly wretched team. By all rights, your decisions tonight should've gotten each of you killed."

Rhiannon closed her eyes and wrestling with the wave of shame that threatened to overtake her. She should've done more, somehow, to protect him. But even as the guilt brought tears to her eyes, she knew better. It didn't do any good to think of that now. There was no point in looking back. She had to focus on what she could do now.

"Where can we take him?" Rhiannon demanded. "Back to the

village? He needs help. Who can help him?"

Mitali hesitated, studying Martin and Rhiannon in turn, then shook her head. "No, the Naga will not aid him. I know you find this an unacceptable response, but that is the truth. He has no clan of his own. I do not know who would care for him. I am not sure what you should do."

Rhiannon felt panic itching at the edges of her mind, threatening to take over. It had been such a long and heavy night. All she wanted to do was to have something work out easily and safely so that she could stop being so afraid. She needed somebody else to come up with the answers.

I have answers. . . a small, distant voice crackled in the back of her mind. Rhiannon tried to ignore it. Her exhaustion made it hard.

Don't be stubborn, little fleshling, the cold sighed. *You will be, of course, but if you're going to keep me here you have to learn to trust me eventually.*

Rhiannon hesitated, considering this. It was true. She'd kept the cold so that she could help Martin, and here it was offering to assist her. Perhaps she needed to give it a chance.

Mitali hissed. "Rhiannon, you cannot be serious. It is one thing to hold the wild magic captive and another to allow it to guide you! Who knows what treachery it may have in store?"

"Like when you kidnapped me and left Martin to die?"

Rhiannon shot back.

Fleshling, there is no time for this. The one before you is well known to me, to all the thread. The power insisted, rushing to be heard. *I understand now who you are. If you had told me that this was your companion, I would not have fought you so. We have been waiting for you.*

What? Rhiannon thought in surprise. *But why?*

"Rhiannon please!" Mitali sounded desperate. "This is not right! This is not how he would've wanted you to find out."

"Mitali, stop it!" Rhiannon snapped, glaring at the Naga and putting walls of fire around her brain. "Stay out of my head!"

Mitali swung her sword in rage, taking a notch out of the tree beside her. "I cannot help it! It is how we are. Much like you cannot seem help being a precocious, wretched fool. Martin would not—"

"You don't get a vote! You left him to die!" Rhiannon shouted back. "I said I was going to save Martin, and I'm not going to let you stop me."

What do I do? Rhiannon thought to the cold while glaring at Mitali. *Quick!*

Don't forget to breathe. The cold did not wait any longer.

The feeling was nauseating, a worm of cold slithering through her and jerking her arm forward before she could stop it. Mitali lurched to yank Martin away, but not quick enough. Rhiannon's hand touched Martin's arm, and he began to turn soft and white as though dissolving into snow. Rhiannon panicked for a moment, but then realized that she, too, was dissolving. Her body was gone, separated into the flecks of white. Mitali was there, staring in horror, but the details of the snake were blurring and softening. It wasn't really like seeing, anymore, more that Rhiannon could feel her shape. She could feel for miles. The trees, the mountains, the animals surging through the brush, it was all there like a map of shapes in her mind.

In the next moment, she was flying away, leaving Mitali behind.

Effortlessly she whooshed through the world, zig-zagging and cartwheeling through the forest with a freedom that she had never imagined. The landscape shifted and swelled around her, but nothing got in her way. She didn't slow down for anything. It was like she was moving through the rocks and plants that were before her.

This is who I am, the thought came through the wild delight. Rhiannon understood. The magic she had was not just cold. She had trapped a winter wind inside of her, untamable and bright.

Rhiannon wanted to speak but found she had no mouth, no body. At this moment, she was simply a part of the wind. Still, she felt more alive than she ever had. All she wanted to do was stay in this place, flowing and dancing over the world, free and wild forever. Rhiannon threw on the breaks, scrambling back from the feelings of joy that were distracting her. She thought, *How did you do this? You were trapped!*

You gave me permission, flesh creature. The wind snapped viciously, leaving a frost in its path through the jungle. *I simply took the opportunity. Don't be so afraid! Why not just enjoy this moment?*

Rhiannon struggled. Her fear is what kept her strong, yet it was so tempting to let go. She struggled to bring her senses to the forefront, watching where they were carefully. The feeling of the world was changing, the wild jungle falling away to a body of water. She couldn't feel anything beneath the surface. It felt like the wind was skirting the edge of the sea, trying to stay close to shore.

Where is Martin? Rhiannon thought.

The one you call Martin is with us, safe in the wind. The wind replied. *We are going to the largest city of this world. Friends of Martin are hiding there.*

Hub? Rhiannon thought.

You've heard of it, then! Here I was thinking you were completely ignorant of our world. The wind seemed pleased, but in a snide sort of way.

It's not my fault! I've only been here for a day.

That explains quite a lot.

Rhiannon's temper flared. She considered wresting back control from the cold. It was probably shallow enough here that they could swim, and she would feel a lot better if she was in control. It was just a matter of pushing back with her own magic, and even though she wasn't completely sure where her body was, she could imagine the way her spark felt. The magic was still there, burning inside of her. She braced herself, preparing to swim.

Something surged out of the water beneath her. It was so big that Rhiannon darted further up out of fear. A kind of fish with a snout full of fangs surfaced and snapped at the air. The cold laughed at her.

No fleshling can harm you when you are one with me like this. It chided. *Enjoy the ride, Druid. What are you so worried about?*

The answer to that question was longer and more complex that Rhiannon could begin to explain, but she knew the first step. *What were you talking about earlier when you said you were waiting for me? What does that mean?*

You are a Druid from the void, are you not?

No! Rhiannon felt remarkably vindicated. *I don't even know what the void is. I'm from Earth.*

No, I'm afraid that can't be. All Druids come from the same place, the darkness that all of our world avoid, the cold said. Rhiannon did not know how to respond, but she was not given time to find words before her world spun yet again. *But why am I the one to tell you these things? Do you not know the one you carry with you?*

Rhiannon was confused. *Of course, I know him. He's Martin.*

. . He's a friend of my Grandmother's. He's lived in my basement for months.

No, not like that, the wind seemed to be getting frustrated and Rhiannon was quite frankly fed up as well. It was as though they were using the same words to mean completely different things.

What should I know about Martin, then? Rhiannon insisted.

He is not like other fey, the wind replied. *He is alone.*

How do you mean?

The wind sighed and bristled. *Fleshling, this is infuriating. If I had known it would be like talking to a stump I wouldn't have bothered explaining. Perhaps the friends of your Martin can explain to you when we arrive.*

Rhiannon petulantly tried to worm her way after the voice but it curled in on itself. All she could do was fly along in silence and pout. Martin would have to answer for this. It made her feel all sorts of wrong that anyone here had been expecting her.

They were leaving the water behind, and now there was a city beneath them. It was a port town with a sprawling dock along the waterfront. Buildings very similar to the shape and size Rhiannon would expect in her world wedged together to take up as much space as they could. She could feel the shapes of the fey creatures walking the streets. They were remarkable. If she had been surprised by the Naga, it was nothing compared to the bizarre and unfamiliar beings in this place. There seemed to be every combination of myth and legend strolling along the boardwalk, bartering over goods, gossiping on the street corners. Rhiannon noticed that as they passed over, the creatures below seemed to shiver suddenly and look around in surprise. Otherwise, nobody gave them much notice.

They were still rushing forward, but the wind took them in a swirling spiral over and through the city, stalling as they looked for something.

What are you looking for? Rhiannon asked.

I can't let you out just anywhere, can I? The wind sneered. *Or do you want to be captured straight off?*

Rhiannon felt there was no call for that kind of response, but tried to be patient.

Finally, they swooped down into an area where the buildings were so tightly packed that the streets would have barely been wide enough for a single car. There was junk all over the place, piled in heaps and spilling over. As they whooshed through the narrow spaces, there were no fey in sight. The wind jerked sideways into a sliver of an ally between two buildings and stopped.

Rhiannon felt like she had burst out of a box of packing peanuts. She now stood on a paved stretch of road, surrounded by a cloud of white fluffy specks. There was a drift of snow that cradled Martin's limp form.

"Martin!" Rhiannon cried.

Shhh! The wind rebuked sharply, making Rhiannon ring. *Don't be stupid!*

Rhiannon was tired of being told she was stupid. It was not her fault she didn't know what was going on. Still, she didn't have time to argue with the power. She hurried to Martin's side and touched his face. His skin was bitingly cold. When Rhiannon dared to peek at the injury on his leg, her stomach clinched and she quickly looked away. It was not pretty. She had never seen skin that particular shade of eggplant.

Rhiannon realized she was up to her knees in snow, soaking through her jeans, but it didn't feel cold to her. Strange.

She stood up and looked around the ally, hoping for an obvious sign. There was no one around, and no doors to the buildings on either side of them. Everything seemed abandoned.

You said there would be help here! Rhiannon thought, her heart thudding quicker in her chest. The panic was making it hard to think straight. *There's nobody here!*

Be thankful that you are a Druid, fleshling, or I would not be so patient with you. Not everything happens in an instant! The cold prickled down her spine, sending goosebumps through her limbs. Rhiannon shuddered and tried to reach the itchy spots it left on her back. She stomped her foot, refusing to be cowed.

You brought me here. You told me to trust you. Now fix this!

As you wish, the cold snapped sarcastically.

The squiggly feeling happened again as the cold shifted inside her, surging down her leg and escaping from her toes. A line of bright, white frost sparked into being between the cracks in the cobbles and skittered off in a trail. It led to the deadened wall at the back of the ally.

What was that for? Rhiannon grumbled.

Just follow the trail, fleshling. The cold seemed exhausted and impatient. *You're really quite a nuisance, aren't you?*

My name is Rhiannon, not fleshling. Rhiannon snapped back.

And I am not simply 'cold' or 'power', yet here we are. If you'd like, you may call me The Northern Wind.

Rhiannon blinked, suddenly realizing that the thing inside of her was more than she'd previously considered. She considered apologizing, but Rhiannon was having none of that. This was not the time for Rhiannon screwed her mouth up and resolved to try and figure it out later. She gave one last look to Martin. Even though she was only turning her back on him for a second, it was nerve-wracking, as though he were going to be gone when she turned back around. She followed the frost trail to the wall.

As far as Rhiannon could tell, the wall was just a wall. It was brown brick, unevenly laid and filthy. Rhiannon looked around uncertainly. This felt stupid.

Oh my goodness, must I do everything? The cold derided, and sent a tendril of cold down Rhiannon's arm again, jerking it towards the wall.

Stop it! Rhiannon gritted her teeth and clenched her fist. Her magic flared hot in her blood, shoving the cold back up her arm and stopping the gesture so that it was little more than a twitch. The cold hissed at her angrily.

What? I'm helping! It snarled.

Just tell me what to do! I am not your puppet!

The cold squirmed angrily inside of its prison, feeling furious. It was trying! It had been proud of what a good job it had been doing helping the stupid little Druid, but nothing seemed to be good enough. Every time it tried something to be useful to it, the little fleshling just wanted it to do something even harder and more unfamiliar. Tell her what to do? It wasn't even sure how they were communicating in the first place! But what choice did it have but to try?

Okay. The cold thought, using the vessel's voice. *Do you see the symbols in the bricks? The wild magic woven into it?*

Rhiannon stared at the brown muddy wall and her eyebrows knitted together. *No.* She thought.

The cold nearly screamed. *This is why I just need to do it!*

No! Rhiannon thought stubbornly.

While we are arguing about this, the Martin is dying!

Rhiannon whipped back around to look at Martin's limp form laying in the melting snowdrift. Her fear made a lump in her throat. Letting her fist go loose, she turned back to the wall, resolved.

Fine. Do it.

She would never get used to that awful feeling of a worm crawling through her body to dig into her limbs. The cold pulled her hand up to the wall and yanked it roughly from brick to brick as it traced out a symbol. Rhiannon had to wince, closing her eyes and fighting the urge to yank back control from the power. The tickling, stinging feeling was worse than the time she'd had a cavity filled.

And then it was over.

Rhiannon pulled her hand to her chest and opened her eyes. There was a red door. She could also see the bricks. She blinked rapidly. It made her dizzy to look at it, but her brain somehow made sense of it. The two things were simultaneously true, the door and the wall, existing in the same space at the same time. She did not want to admit that it was pretty cool.

Rhiannon could see a symbol drawn on the door. It looked like a teardrop with a stem, filled with a network of lines.

Well? Are you going to knock? The cold thought.

Okay. Rhiannon replied, but her mouth was dry. The wind's thoughts were fresh in her mind. They had been waiting for her. . .

who was they? And if they were on the other side of the door, what did they expect from her?

Rhiannon tried to tell herself that this was nothing, that she had been through so much tonight that knocking on a strange door with no knowledge of who or what was on the other side was nothing to be afraid of, but her body did not listen. She glanced toward the alley. Martin was too sick to move, much less to help her or even look up with his typical, comforting, sidelong smirk. It was up to her, now. It had always been up to her, really, but before someone had always been watching. When they were watching it was easier. She was performing for them, and it was easy to be brave because she couldn't let them know how sacred she actually was. Now that she was alone, this small, simple task was going to end her.

Her greatest fear was that she was secretly too afraid to do anything after all.

Rhiannon, the cold said gently in her voice, *it will be alright.*

Rhiannon's knuckles bruised on the door as she rapped it, her blush blazing hot in her cheeks. *I don't need you to tell me that!* Rhiannon thought back, ignoring the gratitude she felt.

Fine, fine. . . The cold thought back wearily. Rhiannon nearly replied, but she was distracted when the door swung open.

. . .

There was a clock ticking somewhere. The walls were mostly

bookshelves, filled with spines of every shape and color. However, the back wall was plated with copper reaching from floor to ceiling. It billowed towards them so that Rhiannon feared they would burst like the walls of a submarine gone too deep. A stairwell twisted off in the corner. Furniture in the large, open room seemed placed with no real design or purpose. Couches and armchairs slanted at odd angles around several squat tables. There was also an impressively tall, well-loved cat tree in the corner, but no cat. That was normal, though. Cats could be evasive.

Rhiannon tapped her fingers against each other. Although she sat in a soft, baby blue armchair, she felt enormously uncomfortable and frankly a bit bored. For the first time since she'd been sucked out of her bedroom, she had a moment to miss her cell phone. The train of thought trailing off from this idea brought in memories of home and a twist of guilty discomfort in her gut, so she quickly distracted herself by picking at the stitching in the upholstery.

"They don't like that. At least, not when I do it."

"Sorry" Rhiannon said, stopping quickly. She glanced at her host, watching his examination of Martin for a moment, then quickly away. There didn't seem to be anyone else here and he was not what she had expected. Whatever Rhiannon had been imagining, she was a bit letdown by this little, gloomy looking man. Although Rhiannon was short for fourteen, the man came just to her eyes. His face looked like someone had pinched in the sides and pulled down so that he was perpetually frowning. His dark hair and beard had probably been trimmed and groomed about a month ago, but had clearly lacked any sort of attention lately.

But he had a voice like she couldn't believe. She could've cuddled up in that voice on a rainy day with a mug of cocoa. The owner of it just happened to look like a stray animal that had been left out in the storm. She found it a lot harder to be obstinate towards his directions when they were offered in soft, warm tones.

They had dragged Martin to a vermillion chaise lounge and he had been poking a prodding Martin for quite some time without much notice for Rhiannon. She'd winced and stopped watching when he'd started jabbing the gaping wound on his leg experimentally. Now he straightened up and looked back at her. "Are you sure you didn't do something to him? He wasn't like this when he left."

Her stomach lurched at the accusation. "Of course, I didn't!" Rhiannon said. "It was a monster that attacked us! We were in the jungle and—"

"Wait," the man said, holding up a hand that stopped the flow of her words immediately. "Don't use the 'M' word."

"Oh. . ." Rhiannon said, with the feeling that she had missed the top step in a flight of stairs. "I'm sorry."

"You didn't know," he said, shrugging.

"Listen, what's your name?" Rhiannon asked, steering for a safer ground.

"What's yours?"

"What? Um. Rhiannon," she said. It felt a bit like he was batting her around like a piece of string.

The man she was speaking to smiled for the first time and it was the most unpleasant thing Rhiannon had ever seen. His eyes didn't change, his lips just pulled back to lift his cheeks slightly. "You're going to have to do better than that."

"What do you mean?" Rhiannon said. Her heartrate spiked. Something in her primitive brain, she recognized that sort of smile and was ready to bolt for the door if he so much as twitched an eyebrow.

With a moment of realization, his expression drooped once more. Rhiannon's feeling of fear evaporated in the same moment, smoothed by his buttery soft voice. "You're safe here, of course, but that was too easy. You're from the void, aren't you?"

Rhiannon sat up a little straighter. "Hey, what do you mean by that? What's the void, anyway?"

"They call me lots of things." He tilted up his chin to scratch under his beard. She blinked at him, feeling agog again. Talking to him made Martin feel like a walk in the park comparatively.

"It doesn't matter, of course," he continued, "I find names tiresome. But if you want me to call you Rhiannon, I will."

"Yes," Rhiannon said. "and. . . what do you want me to call you?" She had wanted to finish that sentence with a thousand different questions that actually mattered more, but she could not quite bring herself to. She squirmed with frustration at how he'd managed to corner her into inane conversation when there were big, looming questions taking up so much space in her brain.

He did not actually smile at her, but in the pause Rhiannon knew that a grin was there. It just couldn't be bothered to show up. "Cat," he said.

Rhiannon compulsively glanced at the cat tree but refused to think the thought that suggested itself. Clearly, he was a human, if a very odd one. "Okay. . . Cat, will you tell me, where are we?"

"No," Cat yawned, showing all his teeth and curling his tongue spectacularly. When he'd smacked his mouth a few times, he continued. "They'll be home soon, anyway. I'm sure they'd rather be in charge of things like that. I would probably lose my tail for spilling secrets too soon."

He's totally actually a cat. Rhiannon thought, trying to surreptitiously see if he had a tail dangling behind him. She couldn't see anything, but maybe it was just tucked inside his pants? She shook her head at herself in embarrassment. It was none of her business what was down his pants.

He's a Bakeneko, the cold thought.

"A what?" Rhiannon asked aloud, forgetting herself in her own excited curiosity.

"My tail." Cat repeated. He had returned to Martin's side and was inspecting the wound in his leg now. He did not look up as he said, "So, did he tell you why you're here, then?"

Electric hope surged her forward in her chair, but a groan erupted from behind the copper plates on the wall. It bellowed through the room like some sort of infernal beast. Rhiannon yelped and jumped out of the chair, darting closer to Martin and Cat. The dour man sighed, somehow looking even more put out. "You get used to it after a while, in a manner."

The copper plates on the wall buckled backwards, sinking into the wall like someone had grabbed them from the opposite side of the wall and pulled. It looked like a funnel going off into nothingness. The sounds of metal bending out of place was still rattling in her ears, but she could hear voices coming down the passage.

"I *told* you this was a mistake, Ainsel!" Came a warbling, ancient voice. "You are going to get us in terrible trouble if you keep this up. We may be part of the resistance but our risks must be *calculated!* Please, allow me to advise you before you speak up next time."

"I know, I know," The lilting whine could only belong to a child.

There was a steady clipping noise, like a woman's heels on

tile. Rhiannon imagined a trio coming closer, the elegant woman, the child, and the old man. She braced herself to see them as the noises neared the mouth of the dark cave.

"I won't always be able to cover for you, you know!" The elderly warble continued. "If they become too suspicious, everything we have worked for will come crashing down. Crashing down!"

The light revealed two figures, a small ephemeral girl with eyes too large for her face, and a satyr. The half-goat man was elderly, with a portly belly and graying fur on his haunches. A pair of tiny specitcals perched on his wide, flat nose. He balked at the sight of Rhiannon.

"Ainsel, stay back!" He chirped, placing a hand on the girl's shoulder.

"Why?" Ainsel asked, peering around the room curiously. "What's Cat done this time?"

"Hi," Rhiannon said nervously. She held up a hand in a half salute, half wave that felt awkward and formal. She quickly dropped the gesture.

"Cat!" The satyr said harshly. "Who is this? What's going on? You know better than to open the door!"

But the man who had been standing beside Rhiannon was gone. Rhiannon looked around anxiously just in time to see a black and white blur of fur darting up the stairs. The satyr groaned, glaring wickedly after him, then turned his beady eyes back to Rhiannon.

"Well? You'll have to explain yourself. Who are you? How did you find us?"

"I'm. . ." Rhiannon should've planned this out. She felt like from his expression she only had seconds to give him a good enough reason not to throw her back in the streets. "I brought Martin!" she blurted out.

"Martin?" Ainsel said. Her eyes seemed to swell to take up even more space in her pale, cherubic face. "Where is he?"

"Oh dear," The satyr said. He clip-clopped across the room quickly to where Martin laid. He did not touch him, but his hands hovered inches above his limp form, looking at him like the shattered pieces of a priceless Ming vase. "What happened to him?"

Rhiannon froze. Visions of blood and the animals' corpses made her stomach heave unpleasantly, though. She squeezed her eyes shut. A little hand slipped into hers and she looked in surprise down at the girl beside her.

"It's okay!" Ainsel chirped. The girl smiled sheepishly up at her.

Rhiannon found herself smiling back. The hand in her palm was warm and soft. The girl couldn't be older than six or seven, with fine, smooth blonde hair falling in a curtain around her face. Rhiannon knew that things were a long way from being okay, but she found that she wanted them to be okay for this child's sake.

"Okay," Rhiannon said. She took a deep breath and looked back up to Bona. "We were attacked. The mon. . . the creatures, they got their claws in him. Literally, the claws were stuck in his leg and I had to. . ." Rhiannon remembered the sounds and smells and felt a wave of threaten to overtake her. She squeezed Ainsel's hand. The blood in her clothes was getting dry and crunchy. She made herself keep talking, trying to keep her mind elsewhere. "They were like wolves or bears or something. . ."

"Fenrir?" The satyr said, the concern in his expression deepening. "But they only live in the wooded areas. There's nothing like that for miles. Where were you? When did this happen?"

Rhiannon shrugged, struggling to do her best. "We were in the jungle. He started to sing this song, and it was like. . . like the whole world was going to break from sadness. Then he passed out and I brought him here. Can you help him? Please?"

The satyr sighed through his large noes, his bottom lip curling out disapprovingly. "Oh, you stupid fox," he muttered. "Alright, let's do our best then. Ainsel, go fetch water. You're his Druid, yes, girl?" The satyr looked at Rhiannon over his spectacles. Ainsel darted off through a door Rhiannon hadn't noticed before.

"I'm not *his*." Rhiannon said stubbornly, but she looked away. He snorted, reeking of pretentious disapproval.

"Thought as much. He was always going on about another one of you and it turns out that as usual he's managed to do everything backwards and sideways. From where I'm standing you hardly seem up for the task. Well, for what it's worth, I don't think that his Goddess would let him die even if he flung himself off a building, though the Source knows he's thought of trying it a time or two." From somewhere the satyr pulled a pair of scissors. He carefully cut away the fabric around the wound, revealing a truly gruesome rainbow of grit and gore. Rhiannon sat down on the floor. She was afraid she was going to faint.

"Oh lovely," the satyr sighed, giving her a frown. His lip protruded about an inch. "Really, girl? You're this flimsy? I'm surprised you made it through a Fenrir attack if this is all you can stand. What good are you going to be to us, then? May as well have left you in the void, if this is all you're worth."

The words stung at Rhiannon's pride, but she was too busy pressing her eyes into her knees and breathing to do more than think angrily at him. *If you'd been through what I've been through in the last 24 hours, you wouldn't be so smug right now. . .*

A feeling of cool relief spread across her face, like someone pressing a soft, damp cloth on her cheeks. The power was doing what it could for her. *Don't listen to him, fleshling,* it said to her. *He's waited for you a long time. It's not going to be easy for you to impress him, but I've seen what you're made of. You're worth more than he can imagine.*

Stop saying this stuff, Rhiannon begged. It was souring her stomach to feel so on the edge of something huge and frightening. She just wanted to sleep. First, though, she had to make sure that Martin was alright, though. She picked up her head, fighting the wooziness.

"Is Martin going to be alright?" Rhiannon asked. She looked up at the satyr, glad she could not see the work he was doing on Martin's leg from her position on the floor.

The satyr spared her a glance. Although it seemed impossible with how furrowed his forehead already was, his brows sunk deeper. "Well, yes. I suppose. But you're in no condition to help now, I see that."

"I can take her upstairs." Rhiannon felt a rush of endorphins at the voice of the Cat, coming as if from nowhere. She turned to see that he had slunk back in at some point and was standing there, bored, as if he'd never left. "She needs to sleep."

"Fine. Do that then. I can't be bothered to take care of another child right now. Ainsel is enough for me to worry about."

Rhiannon remembered being hefted into the Cat's arms, and the faint smell of fish and wood smoke before she let herself collapse. The longest day she'd ever lived was finally over.

Chapter Seven
The Truth

Rhiannon was sure it was a dream.

There were plenty of tells. The grass was too green. It was bright and sharp, so much that she could nearly smell it just from the color. The grass stretched endlessly. The world was empty besides the breeze, and she could not feel the wind so much as see it. She followed the thin lines moving through the air across the grass until they reached the trees. They stood in a small circle. That was the point of this place.

She could not remember the walk across the plain, but she must've done it. She stood in the shade of the trees. They were twelve, beautiful, young trees in the flush of spring. Their trunks made an almost perfect circle. Rhiannon went into the open space between them and sat. She tilted her head, looking up at the sky between the soft, new leaves.

It was the feeling of falling backwards, and it did not stop. Where she should have landed on the grass, she continued to fall, and where there had been trees and sky and dirt there was now expansive darkness. It was thick, inky black and she was falling slowly through it. Floating might have been a better word to describe what was happening. It was difficult to tell which way was up and which was down.

She spun slightly, feet and head moving forever towards and away from each other in slow motion. It was what she had always imagined outer space must've felt like. The stars winked into existence filling up the expanse.

Wake up, a voice came through the dark, and Rhiannon's eyes opened.

She was in a bed. The room was cozy, all wood floors and white walls, with a little window that let in yellow afternoon light. She could hear the muffled sounds of a busy city outside. Her heart was pounding.

It had not felt like being asleep. She had felt completely alert and aware. The voice had not been speaking to her, she was certain, and she felt a moment of frustration that she had responded to it without meaning to. There was something else that she was supposed to see, something bigger and more important. Closing her eyes, she willed herself to fall back asleep, but her whole body protested. Nothing about her was even remotely tired anymore. Rhiannon sighed and stared up at the ceiling, replaying the details of the vision.

Something jumped onto the foot of her bed. A patchy black and white cat, mostly bones, stood by her feet. He was looking at her expectantly. When she pushed herself up on her elbows, he began to purr, a sweet and cozy sound that instantly reminded Rhiannon of the man she'd met yesterday. There was no denying who she was looking at.

"Uh, hi, Cat." Rhiannon said.

Cat sat down, squinting at her.

"Listen," Rhiannon continued, propping herself up on her elbows to look at him. "I know that you're actually a person, or at least that you can be a person, and I don't really feel comfortable having you in bed with me. Do you mind?"

There was a moment where the cat looked off and away, staring at seemingly nothing, and then leapt down from the bed as though it had been his intention all along.

"Thank you." Rhiannon said.

The cat meowed from the floor, a soft pleading noise, and sprang up to the small table beside Rhiannon's pillow. Navigating the tiny space around a pile of books and glass of water, he balanced to reach out towards Rhiannon with one white paw.

"Alright, I get it," Rhiannon said, shoving the blankets off of her and sitting up. "You've been sent to get me up, haven't you? Well, I'm up. Happy?"

Cat did not respond, but slipped from the table and padded out of the room without looking back, the white tip of it's dark tail flicking in the air. Rhiannon shook her head, and looked down at herself. Someone had taken off her ratty sneakers, but she was still wearing the same jeans and t-shirt she'd had on for two days now, complete with blood stains. They were vile. She felt completely disgusting. What she really wanted, most of all, was to clean up. Maybe they had a shower here?

She swung out of the bed and the floorboards moaned in protest. Rhiannon winced and tried to tip-toe across the room as quietly as possible to no avail. The whole house probably knew she was up. When she got to the door, the satyr was there waiting for her. He had a towel in his arms.

"Good morning, Druid," he said, though his tone sounded as though it were not. "We will be dining downstairs in half an hour. During this time, you may use the bath and dress in the clothes we have found you. They might not fit perfectly but it's the best we can do under the circumstances."

The satyr thrust the towel at Rhiannon and pointed down the hall. "The bath is through that door. Please do not be late for the meal."

"Hey, wait!" Rhiannon called after the satyr who had already started to walk off. He paused and turned back. "How's Martin?"

Again, the satyr looked at her oddly, little mountains and valleys forming in his brow. "He is fine. His body more or less repairs itself when given half a chance to. All I really had to do was clean out the poison and make sure he stayed alive long enough for his magic to start working. It is odd how often things like this happen."

"Things like what?" Rhiannon pressed.

The satyr waved his hands. "Martin is either the luckiest fey who has ever been or the unluckiest. The number of times he has *nearly* died are innumerable. I am not sure what it is that compels him to behave as he does, putting his life in constant risk, but I suspect that his Goddess is pushing him to the edge and keeping him there. I suspect that it is because he must."

"What do you mean, Goddess?" Rhiannon was practically on top of the satyr now, clutching the towel to her chest. "And can you tell me what people mean by the void? And I keep hearing that I'm here for something, but what? I thought it was all just an accident." The satyr's lip bulged forward petulantly as he squinted at her.

"You do not know?" He asked, obviously concerned. "He did not tell you?"

"Nobody tells me anything." Rhiannon said, shaking her head. "Please! I've been dying to know more about this world. Even the wild magic that I caught won't tell me anything about— "

"That you *caught?*" The satyr said, hands suddenly clasping Rhiannon's shoulders. "You are not telling me that you already carried wild magic, are you? Are you mad? How reckless can you be!"

Oh fiddlesticks, Rhiannon thought, realizing her mistake. "Never mind that right now." Rhiannon said quickly.

"Let's just be glad that it left you without consuming you

whole, yes? You very well could have died." The satyr grumbled, shaking his head. The fey had a long, wispy beard that was just clung to his chin. It quivered with his disapproval.

Rhiannon swallowed, looking deep into the satyr's bespectacled eyes. She could see how afraid he was. "I. . . It's fine." Rhiannon said. "I have it under control."

His eyes narrowed. "What do you have under control?"

"The magic. . . I mean, the wind. The North Wind." Rhiannon said.

"Are you suggesting you brought it into this house?" The satyr stammered, clutching Rhiannon's shoulders roughly in his hands. His face flushed quickly, turning a shade of magenta that Rhiannon found alarming. The satyr struggled. He started to speak, then stopped, then shook his head. He let go of Rhiannon's shoulders and began to pace, mumbling to himself. "What could Martin have possibly taught her so that she thought this was a good idea? What could he have taught her so that she was even capable of it? Why, I haven't heard of anyone—"

Rhiannon's temper blazed. "Martin didn't teach me anything!" Rhiannon blurted out. The satyr stopped short, snorting sharply at her.

"Don't be ungrateful to your tutor. The fact that you can hold wild magic at all is proof that he has been an excellent teacher, although a foolhardy one."

"He didn't!" Rhiannon insisted. "He didn't teach me a single thing! We came here by accident! But you know what, I'm not sorry about the wild magic. I had to do it. Mitali left him for dead and abducted me, so yes! I used the magic to save him, and guess what? I figured it out on my own! I don't know anything about this stuff, but I did it anyway because I had to. I had to." She repeated, as though hearing it again would convince the old goat.

"You are. . . quite a foolish little thing." The satyr whispered. His expression was something between awe and horror. "Perhaps Martin is not the only one being protected by the Goddesses, although Source knows they must be desperate. . . Well. My name is Bona." He said suddenly, looking at Rhiannon shrewdly.

Rhiannon blinked in surprise. "Oh! Um. I'm Rhiannon."

"Rhiannon." He repeated then he nodded, turning for the stairs. "Well, Rhiannon, come downstairs soon. Martin has insisted that we must eat. Twenty minutes. Go clean up."

Rhiannon could've taken much longer in the hot tub of water, but reluctantly rushed herself through the process of cleaning the grime off her skin. It felt like washing off the trauma from last night. She put on the clothes Bona had given her. It was a cream colored, loose fitting dress that reached her knees. It was not to her taste at all, but it was better than wearing the stinking clothes that had come through the forest with her.

She was at the top of the stairs when she stopped. Voices were floating up from the floor below, Martin and Bona having some sort of mumbled conversation. If she strained her ears she could hear what they were talking about. She crouched, trying to catch more of their words.

"But you've done her a great disservice!" Bona was speaking quickly, voice following an indignant lilt. "She is here, in our world, with no idea what the rules are. And there *are* rules, Martin! You seem to think that you can do whatever you'd like with no concern for the consequences to the rest of us. An untrained Druid with wild magic? At this time? You know that the High Council is demanding a move away from the untamed ways. As well they should, may I add! They might be a batty bunch of loons but on that front, I agree with them whole heartedly. This will not be unnoticed! What were you thinking?"

"So, you think this was the plan?" Martin retorted. "Nothing about this has gone like I wanted it to, which as you know is par for the course. The plans of mortals, eh? It's fine, though. If she's still walking and talking normally then we can assume that the power must be relatively benign. Not all thread is corrupt, and I'm sure I can teach her—"

"You don't know that! You don't know that at all!" Bona interrupted. Rhiannon could imagine his finger waggling under Martin's smug grin. "It could be waiting. It could be toying with her. It might already be too late for her to send it away!"

Rhiannon felt defensive anger bubble inside of her. *Stay calm,* the wind thought to her. *It will do no good to lash out at him.*

How can he say that about you, though? Rhiannon snapped back.

Their conversation was interrupted as Cat came slinking down the stairs behind her in his fur-covered form. Rhiannon froze, mentally begging him not to rat her out. The feline didn't so much as glance at her.

"So, what do you propose, old goat? That we abandon her in the forest? That we light candles and draw runes and try to expel it with old magic? Hm?"

"There's no call for that sort of comment," Bona said stiffly. "I wasn't saying that at all."

"We need her, Bona. You know this, don't you?" Martin said, though the venom had gone out of his voice. He sounded tired. Rhiannon though he was almost begging. "We have to free The Source before the High Council can destroy it. We have to keep the world from falling apart while we do it. Somebody has to care for the lands, or all of the other work will be for nothing."

"I still don't understand why—"

"Excuse me?" Cat chimed in. Rhiannon's stomach turned a somersault. "Perhaps this part can wait just a moment. . ."

"What? Why?" Bona said, flustered.

Rhiannon felt a nervous chill run down her back and she quick-ly straightened, making plenty of noise as she came down the stairs. "Good morning," She said, perhaps too brightly. The dress flounced around her knees as she walked.

"Ah." Said Bona, narrowing his eyes at her. He turned his gaze to the rough looking man sitting on the floor by the table. "How long was she listening?"

Cat's expression was unmoved. "I don't know what you mean."

But Rhiannon found that she didn't really care what Bona or Cat had to say at the moment. Her eyes were fixed on Martin and the bandage around his thigh. She had imagined him pale and weak, but his amber eyes twinkled. He looked absolutely like himself. "Good morning yourself, little love. I hear you braved some fairly terrible events to save me. My gratitude." He bowed his head, twirling his hand in a flourish.

Rhiannon tried to glare at him but her mouth wouldn't co-operate, twitching at the corners. Her angry eyes glinted with mirth. "Yes well. . . Don't let it happen again." She managed. Rhiannon scrunched up her nose and very nearly stuck her tongue out at him, but instead turned away and went to the table, sitting in a chair to wait for food. It felt like the right moment to hug him. She'd never really hugged him before, though. How would she even go about such a thing? She found it was tricky to look at him without her treacherous grin bubbling up. Stupid old fox. . . Who did he think he was, nearly dying and then acting like everything was fine? She smiled to herself, careful to keep her face where he wouldn't see. She was glad he was alright.

Bona stood and clip-clopped to the table himself, sitting across from her. "Rhiannon, I think that we need to discuss—"

"Your options for breakfast!" Martin interrupted. "Come, kitty, help me to the table."

Cat stood and served as a crutch as Martin hobbled towards where the others were sitting. Bona's lip curled and he shook his head. "Really? You obey *his* orders?" The satyr grumbled.

"Ainsel!" Martin called. "Breakfast!"

Ainsel came darting out from the kitchen, beaming and holding a tray barely big enough to hold the five plates crammed onto it. "Breakfast!" She said proudly.

Rhiannon did not laugh, but only because she saw the look on the girl's face and felt that laughing at this would be the same as spitting on a priceless work of art. The food on the breakfast plates looked like something that a six-year-old would come up with, but Ainsel could not have been prouder. It was food that Rhiannon was familiar with, simply mashed together in grotesque combinations. Spaghetti, jelly beans, scrambled eggs, pancakes, sandwich meat, snickerdoodle cookies, canned fish, and mashed potatoes filled the plates in varying ratios. Rhiannon also thought she saw some potato chips on a plate.

Ainsel plopped a dish in front of each of them, obviously having prepared a specific dish for each of her clients. Rhiannon was thankful that hers seemed to be mostly spaghetti with a few eggs and a glob of what was probably strawberry frosting. She tentatively stuck her finger in it to taste the bright pink fluff. She was right.

Bona looked uncertainly at his plate, a single pancake topped with a slice of lunch meat, poking it with a finger. "Gilly, can't we just eat our normal food? All of this just seems so. . . excessive." He asked.

Martin, who had gotten jelly beans and crumbled cookies on a bed of potatoes and frosting, eyed Bona's plate thoughtfully. "Well, Bona, if you really feel that's what you must do then you're welcome to it. By all means, don't let me stop you." Martin said, reaching out and swapping the two plates. Bona did not argue as he quickly went off to the kitchen.

Cat was perfectly happy with his plate of mashed potatoes and canned fish. Ainsel, who had given herself a little of everything, was digging in with relish. Rhiannon picked up a fork and dug into the spaghetti. It wasn't bad, even if it was a little stale.

"Do you like it? Martin brought it back for us for Special

Occasions," The way Ainsel said the words, Rhiannon could hear the capitalization. "You get to eat this all the time in the void, right?" Ainsel said around a mouthful of rainbow colored food.

"What?" Rhiannon said, puzzled.

"Earth. Remember, Ainsel, it's called Earth." Martin said. Rhiannon nearly dropped her fork. Why would they call Earth the void? She turned to Martin, question already in the back of her throat, but stopped at his expression. He was looking at her beseechingly. Rhiannon closed her mouth and sighed, turning back to her breakfast.

"Right. Yes. Sorry." Ainsel said. "On Earth. So, do you? Eat like this?"

"Oh. Um. . . " Rhiannon paused, giving the bite of eggs and spaghetti a thoughtful look. "Something like that."

"Ah, my dear, let us be completely honest. No creature, not on any plane of existence, has the opportunity to dine like this, Ainsel, my sweet. Your cooking is one of a kind." Martin chimed, taking a bite of the pancake that he clearly relished. The little girl beamed like sunrise.

Bona returned holding a piece of something square and brown that Rhiannon suspected was as tasteless as the forest fruit was, although the texture seemed crunchier. He was chewing happily and sat down at the table alongside the others as they ate their meals. "So," Bona said when he'd swallowed. "Rhiannon, I was saying that I think you need to know more about—"

"Bona, please!" Martin interrupted, rolling his eyes. "Must we have such plain conversation over the breakfast table? Breakfast is a sacred time of day!"

"Martin. . . " Rhiannon said stiffly. "Why are you trying so hard to keep me in the dark?"

There was the slightest hiccup in Martin's demeanor, a look he gave that was just a bit too sad, too real. Then he grinned again. Rhiannon's frustration spiked, but she was relieved in a way. It was her familiar Martin, even if she did hate him a little bit.

"I cannot tell a lie, sweet little love. I simply wanted to spare you as long as I could as a favor to an old friend. I'm sorry," Martin said shrugging. He turned to Bona and held his hands wide. "The floor is yours."

Bona sighed, and removed his glasses, polishing them with a napkin. "Really, Martin, all of this fuss. It's not as though I'm going to hurt the poor girl," he grumbled, returning his glasses to his face. "Well, I hardly blame you. It seems as though she's been through a great deal. Child, I have questions about what you've experienced since you've arrived in our world, but there are more pressing issues."

"Yes!" Rhiannon said, hugely relieved. "Please, I need you to explain what everyone is talking about. What am I supposed to do here? What are people expecting from me? How do you guys even know anything about me?"

Bona shook his head stubbornly. "Alas, you must wait."

"Seriously?" Rhiannon wailed.

"Yes! The explanation of what you have been thrown into the middle of will take time, time we might not have if you are a corrupted vessel!" The satyr insisted, poking the table with one stubby finger to punctuate his point. "The first thing we must do is to ensure that you are safe from the wild magic inside of you. My girl, are you sure you're in complete control? Do you have the proper wards set? It is hard for me to believe that you are properly focused on maintaining a safe boundary when you're acting so silly and passionate in what should be a calm and reasonable conversation! The wild magic inside of you could lash out and destroy us all at a moments notice!"

Foolish goat, the North Wind chimed in.

Finally! Thank you. I'm sick of this guy's attitude, Rhiannon thought back, taking a moment to look away from Bona. *What should I tell him? He seems to think you're basically evil incarnate. We have to fix this.*

Why bother? He won't understand anyway. His view of magic is a mess, a hybrid of old and new that misses the truth of both. The power was sneering at Bona.

Okay, but you heard him. I won't learn anything until we get him to calm down about us working together. You're trapped, right?

Rhiannon felt a lurch in her ribs and the air in her chest stung as it turned cold. Rhiannon gasped and gripped the edge of the table, suddenly concerned. She could feel the power thrashing inside of her, suddenly pushing hard against her body to get free. *Hey!* Rhiannon snapped, and on reflex she pushed her heat and anger back down onto the cold, her imagination breathing white-hot flames at the writhing cold. The wind melted quickly back into submission.

See? You're getting better at that. The North Wind thought at her.

"What's going on?" Bona asked.

Rhiannon looked back up at satyr, who was glaring at her suspiciously. She shook her head. "Sorry, I was just having a little talk with the wind. I think I've still got it under control, although I can't help but wonder if it's not taking it easy on me."

I'm not. The cold sulked.

"Excuse me?" Bona said, leaning forward. "You were talking to it? To the wild magic?"

"Er. . . right, the wild magic." Rhiannon corrected herself.

"You were talking to it?" Bona repeated.

"Yes?" Rhiannon tried. "Is that weird?"

"Child! I don't honestly believe it's possible!" Bona blustered, beard twitching madly as he shook his head. "Why, wild magic is one of the most destructive forces here in our world. Some fey can channel it, bend it to their will, but unless they release it quickly the magic consumes them and devours their very soul. You cannot *talk* to wild magic. It would be like talking to a rock! Or a hammer!"

Bona seemed pleased with this comparison, but the air around Rhiannon's skin began to steam slightly as her body temperature dropped. "Oh. . ." Rhiannon said, mentally begging the cold to calm down.

Fine. Let me talk to him. It growled in her voice.

I don't think that's a good idea. Rhiannon thought back. The power felt like a dog growling from its hackles. *You're not allowed to hurt him.*

I can't hurt him unless you want me to. The cold reminded her. *Besides, I just want to talk to him. Let me use your voice.*

Rhiannon pondered this for a moment. It did seem a little unfair that the power couldn't speak for itself. After all, clearly Bona had some ideas that weren't correct. . . *Fine.* Rhiannon relented.

Bona saw a shiver run through Rhiannon and a blinding white light, like sun shining off of snow, flashed in her eyes for a moment. The small girl suddenly held herself differently, her shoulders down and back, head held regally aloft. She looked at least an inch taller. She smiled and Bona felt a chill run down his spine. "Rhiannon?" He asked.

"Yes," She replied, "but not at the moment. She has allowed me this audience to explain what you seem to have forgotten about my people, you misguided goat."

The fey all tensed. Ainsel slipped out of her chair to duck underneath the table. Martin glared. "What did you do to her?" He growled.

Rhiannon, who was not Rhiannon, turned to Martin and her face softened. The smile he received was sweeter than anything Rhiannon could muster on her best day. He felt his hackles rising. "Dear fey called Martin, you are the last who knows the truth. Do not fear for the girl. I would not harm this vessel for the world. She is, as you know, the last hope of both our kinds. I am honored to be with her. But you!" Rhiannon snapped, turning a frigid look back to Bona.

"Me?" He said, fear and surprise coming onto his face. "But I'm not the one who trapped you! I wanted her to free you, to let you go!"

"Indeed. And you wanted her to believe any number of degenerate lies about what I am. Have you noticed what a lovely conversation we're having now?" Rhiannon said sharply. She barred her teeth through every word as though imagining the reasons creatures grew fangs. "You filthy, worthless fleshlings have completely forgotten what you were even made for. My own people, the birds of the snow, are nearly gone. There are perhaps five left in The Otherworld! The

Devastation consumed whole mountain ranges! Of course, I wander! Of course, I seek partnership! What are we for, but that? Yet I find no one to be my partner, only those wanting to wrestle me into submission, abuse me for their own ends, and then expel me like I am nothing more than a useless tool. Perhaps a bit like a hammer, yes? Or a crude rock?"

Bona moved back in his chair, holding his hands together in front of him as though cradling something small. Although his fingers were shaking, he began to twitch them, small sparks of green light flying. Martin reached out to stop him.

"Wait!" Martin said, "Rhiannon is in there!"

"Yes. She is. And I would not harm her for the world." The girl said, placing a gentle hand on her own cheek. "When I came into her, it's true, I wanted to consume her. I thought she was weak and I was angry. This fleshling, though, she is stronger than anything I've ever seen. She is kinder and braver than any fey I've ever encountered. She did not want anything from me but the chance to survive, the chance to save you, sweet Martin. I am with her as much by my own choice as by her own will now. Where idiot beasts like *that* one try to force us into their own image," Rhiannon gave a pointed glare to Bona, "forgetting how we and the fey were crafter as two parts of one whole, this creature simply asked me to help her. So yes, I speak to the girl. Hopefully she'll be able to teach you a thing or two about how we spirits work."

Rhiannon nodded firmly, took a deep breath and then collapsed with a sigh, dark hair falling forward in a curtain as her head lolled.

That felt really weird. Rhiannon thought, feeling her brain swim back into control. She had been aware of what her body was doing, but it was like a dream where she was observing her behavior from a little room inside of her head. The feeling of touching her own cheek had surprised her.

I am sorry if it was uncomfortable. The North Wind said, but then withdrew. Rhiannon felt waves of complex emotions radiating from the space where it dwelled inside of her, and she knew it wanted to be alone. She picked up her head and looked around the table.

All of the eyes were staring at her.

"So. . . There's that." Rhiannon said shrugging.

"Amazing." Bona whispered.

The silence hung on. Rhiannon found herself unsure of how to break it.

"Well!" Said Martin brightly, "That was nice."

"Nice?" Bona spat. He gaped at Martin. "Nice! We unearth a whole new dynamic of communication with wild magic and you just call it nice?"

"You know, of course, that it should be called thread? Isn't that right, Rhiannon?"

"Uh. . ." Rhiannon said, furrowing her brow. The North Wind wasn't speaking to her and her own knowledge was fairly limited. Bona didn't give her a chance to figure it out, though.

"Yes, yes, that's another way of thinking!" His shaking beard looked like a little fish squiggling on his chin. "But really, now most fey don't even care to know what's really going on. Thread, wild magic. . . there isn't really a difference. Odd how the wild magic would bring up the Devastation at a time like this, too. You know, Martin, I've been meaning to talk to you about that as well, now that you're back and all."

"Bona. . ." Ainsel said in warning, but the satyr waved her away.

"You see, Martin, we're having a bit of a time trying to convince the High Council to change their tactics in regard to the migration efforts. You understand, don't you? Of course, I believe you, but it's a bit of a struggle to sway the minds of those entrenched in other ways of thinking."

Rhiannon noticed a change in Bona. He picked up the pace of his words, as though trying to build a sort of barricade out of them. She caught the look on Martin's face, and suddenly she wished she understood more of what Bona was saying. Martin was not bothering to hide the stormy expression, his glare glinting hard from under low brows. She didn't understand what was happening, but it was clearly upsetting Martin.

". . . but really, the High Council seems unswayable. We're trying, I swear, but obviously our hands are tied to a certain degree. The Devastation is a problem, everyone knows, but it's difficult to prove why it's happening. I mean, of course, I believe you, Martin! I said so, didn't I? But if we come out too openly against the crusade then suspicions will be aroused and our clans might suffer. We are Speakers, after all, and that comes with a certain responsibility—"

"You're fey first." Martin interrupted. His words halted Bona's flow of words dead. "Were you using all this fuss over the thread as a distraction so I wouldn't know how you'd failed us, Bona?"

Bona stopped as suddenly as if Martin had pulled a knife on him. The satyr wilted under the blighting look Martin was giving him. It seemed as though Bona was done talking for now.

"Martin?" Rhiannon dared to lean towards him, touching his hand. He looked ready to murder, but Rhiannon was oddly unafraid. After all, she had grown up with Bear and Grandma Deedee. Angry looks were part of the package.

Martin held up a hand to stop her, though. His voice rumbled low when he spoke, sizzling through the air so that she felt glued to her chair. "Rhiannon, allow me to explain all of this," He did not look at her as he spoke but kept his vicious eyes on Bona. "This fey is wise and well-learned, a trusted friend of mine, but however much he knows, he is welcome to speak twisted truths. He is free to believe lies and spread them like a disease."

"Martin, I'm not—" Bona said weakly.

Martin stood from the table. "Time is too short to waste on the stories they tell themselves to escape their duty to our world. Come with me, Rhiannon. You will know the truth." He walked towards the stairs, swift purpose elongating his stride. Rhiannon had to spring and scurry to keep up with him.

"Gilly, wait!" Bona hissed after him. "Please don't wake her! It's too much of a risk! She'll—"

"Bona, shut up." Cat drawled. Martin did not bother to look back, and Rhiannon did not dare to do anything but follow his lead exactly.

Martin walked to the door at the end of the hall, Rhiannon on his heels. When he stopped, Rhiannon nearly tripped over herself, but something had shifted in his demeanor. The time he stood staring at the door could've been seconds, but Rhiannon was acutely aware of each tiny sound, each shift in Martin's weight. The man turned to her. He no longer looked like a hurricane of rage, but seemed genuinely afraid.

"Rhiannon. . ." He closed his eyes for a moment. "I am sorry.

I trusted them to do so much while I was away and to find out like this that they're wavering. . . Bona was a good fey. I still believe I can trust him but he's forgotten so much. . ."

"It's cool," Rhiannon said. The words felt tiny and insufficient, but they made him smile a little. He sighed, looking back at the door.

"I didn't really think this through. Now we've committed, and I don't think I could stomach going back downstairs without actually following through." He confessed. "I am sorry, but I do think this is the best choice. I know that she can be. . . difficult. She doesn't know what she's doing, though. Well, she does, but. . . " Martin shook his head and pressed the palms of his hands together, stopping his rambling.

"Rhiannon, I am going to introduce you to my sister." Martin said, trying to center himself. He found himself staring at the wall over Rhiannon's head, unable to make eye contact. He had known that he would have to do this eventually, but now? Everything with Rhiannon was out of order, topsy-turvy. If only Bona hadn't discussed his dealings with the Council perhaps he could have kept his head! Alas, this is where they were. Martin made himself press on. "She is sick. She had a run in with some fey who did not like what she did, who she was, and in response they. . . well, they hurt her very much. She is still in there, but. . ."

"I think I understand." Rhiannon said. Martin looked back at her, the gentleness in her voice making his throat swell. "I mean, I can't understand, but I'll be kind to her, Martin. What's her name?"

"Una." Martin said. He felt the tension go out of his shoulders, and on impulse he reached out and ruffled Rhiannon's black, wild hair. "Thank you, little love. But I must say something else. Everything you see will be true. It might not be true yet, it might not be your truth, but it will be an inarguable truth. I trust her to tell you what you need to know. Please, Rhiannon. I need you to promise that if it becomes too much, you will tell me. Let me get you out of there when you need to go."

I will help. I will know if you need to stop. The cold said with a gravity that made Rhiannon shiver from something unrelated to the temperature.

"Okay." Rhiannon said, taking a deep breath. Whatever was going to happen, it was obviously a big deal. She felt like asking questions would only get in the way. She just had to trust that Martin knew what he was doing. Rhiannon had to fight the bubble of bitter laughter that sparked at that thought. Trust Martin? The silly, shiftless piano teacher that never made any sense at all? But this was not that man. The adult before her was obviously scared, and he was deadly serious. This was the Martin she had always known was there underneath and the reason she hadn't given up on him yet.

"Let's do this." She said.

Martin opened the door.

The room on the other side was a surprise. It was small and painfully bare. The walls were white. The floor was white. There was no decoration and no furniture aside from a large bed, pushed against the middle of the far wall so that there were about five feet on every side of the white, fluffy bed. In the bed was a woman so delicate and perfect that Rhiannon thought for a moment she must be made of porcelain. Her skin was the same nutty shade as Martin's, her hair the faintest blonde that Rhiannon had ever seen. The effect was something of a Baroque period sculpture, the artist capturing the perfect image of frozen serenity.

Everything felt muffled and still. Martin crept to the bedside and knelt. Rhiannon followed. He motioned for her to sit on the bed. Rhiannon hesitated only for a moment. Something told her that this was the last chance she had to turn and flee, to escape whatever would happen when this vision of beauty woke up. Deep down, though, she knew it was already too late. She had to know the truth about this world, even if it changed everything.

Rhiannon sat.

The woman's eyes flashed open with a sharp, sucking breath pulled through her nose. Her eyes were Martin's eyes, the amber color of liquid fire, but these were larger, wider, and full of fear. They fixed on Rhiannon, pupils immediately spreading wide to fill most of the color with darkness.

"Una," Martin said. Una's wide, rabbit gaze ticked to him immediately. His tone was tender, cheerful almost. He was grinning, and looked for all the world like he always did, a playful and silly trickster without a care in the world. Rhiannon was surprised at the pride she felt. He reached out and held out a hand near the woman's face, much like she'd seen people do to stray animals they were trying to connect with.

"Una, it's Gilly." He said again. The woman blinked. Rhiannon was entranced by the way her pupils fluctuated. She tilted her head slightly to tip her cheek into Martin's palm. His smile turned genuine. "You're safe, Una. You're safe."

But Una looked back at Rhiannon, long fair lashes floating up and down over her eyes. Rhiannon's heart beat faster. She tried to relax her body, to seem as gentle and unthreatening as Martin did, but it was hard. She was afraid that if she unclenched her jaw it would start to chatter. There was something about this woman that was scaring her badly, more than much of what she'd seen over the last few days.

"Una," Martin said, pushing the word a little harder to bring her eyes back to him. "this is my friend, Rhiannon. You can tell who she is, yes?"

The slightest nod, the woman's cheek brushing against

Martin's palm.

"You can see what she needs to know?" Martin asked again, speaking lightly, so lightly, like it was all a game. "Can you show her, my rainbow?"

The woman's lips twitched for a moment, the tiniest of smiles as if on instinct before they went slack again, and she nodded once more. Her head turned further towards Martin's hand and she placed the slightest kiss on his palm. "I've missed you, Gilly." Una whispered. She sounded like her voice had rusted over from lack of use.

"I've missed you too, sunset." Martin said, ever so gently running his thumb across her cheek as though even this slight contact might bruise her.

Rhiannon still couldn't let the tension out of her body. Now her shoulders were trembling. Something terrible was going to happen, she could feel it. She flinched at sudden touch to her hand, but saw it was Martin. She met his eyes and saw he was smiling at her now, the same way he'd been looking at Una.

"It will be okay, Rhiannon." Martin said. "I know how it feels to be near her, but you're doing great. Just remember to breathe. Ask your power for help if you need it. I believe that the wild magic will help you."

Rhiannon nodded and looked back at Una. Their eyes locked. The thinnest line of color rimmed her dark pupils now. It was mystifying. The darkness plumed through the barrier of color, bleed-ing outside the lines and filling the whole of Una's eyes. Rhiannon fell into the darkness. All she could see was black.

Chapter Eight

How it Begins

She had been here before. Rhiannon was sure she was awake this time, though. The grass, the wind, the trees in the distance were all immediately familiar. It was an exact replica of her dream from the night before. Rhiannon took a step towards the trees. She put her foot down inside their shade, arriving in the same moment she decided to go.

It was exactly the same as her dream, and it was hard not be frightened by it. Everything from the shapes of the trees to the strange stillness. Although she could not say she felt safe there, she felt that it was right. It felt sacred. She sat in the grass, already knowing how the world would tilt backwards and she would fall into space, staring into a world of tiny winking lights spreading out into infinity. It looked cold, the ever-stretching abyss.

Wake up, came the voice.

This time, Rhiannon watched a brilliant, golden light burst into existence. It exploded, blinding her, but the light softened and Rhiannon was able to look at it more clearly. The light dripped and coiled, but also flickered like fire. It was something between a flame and pool of honey, shining brilliantly. What consumed Rhiannon was the feeling of joy that erupted in her chest. She did not know what it was, but it was beautiful. It felt like a sunrise or a blossoming flower. It was alive and abundant.

Rhiannon felt a pounding noise rise up in her chest. She had to shout, to scream, to sing at the top of her lungs or she would surly explode. With more confidence than she'd ever felt before, she threw her head back and roared. The sound was everything; a chorus of song, a clash of thunder, a howling gale screaming through a canyon, a warbling bird heralding spring. The light chased the sound, dashing beside it to spread through the world. Rhiannon went alongside, flying full tilt. It felt like a race and a dance woven into one.

New things rushed in to meet them, the girl, the light and the noise. She felt it all. She watched mountains and oceans and glaciers spring up as though pulled from clay. She saw light and color and noise rattle through the world. As the fabric of reality took shape, Rhiannon began to name the things she saw. Although the words felt alien in her mouth, each sound was familiar and perfect. These were true names, real and secret beyond measure.

Through all of it, the light darted and played. It danced through creation. The cosmos watched on.

Everything grew, taking on life of its own. Creation began to grow over itself, battling for space that was already spoken for. Rivers flowed where mountains already stood. Forests spread roots to arid deserts. Change followed change. Things began to destroy each other in an effort to consume more space and time for themselves. Rhiannon wailed in anguish as parts of the masterpiece were snuffed out.

The light saw this, and twisted again. It wrung out part of itself, dripping and flickering onto the reality below. Where they landed, sparks flew in a cacophony of color. They were new beings, both belonging to and completing the things from which they had sparked. Rhiannon laughed, delighted. The new sparks were playing freely, dancing with one another, caring for their own little corner of the world in a coordinated dance with the others.

The light danced on, and the world grew. Everything was good so long as there were ones to watch over the world.

The sparks zoomed to tend to their creations, spreading themselves far to care for the ever-expanding world. Rhiannon saw things falling apart, saw regions tearing away again as the guardians of the land could no longer protect the full domain. Rhiannon looked for the golden light, the mother of them all, and willed it to give aid. The golden light seemed oblivious to this. The sparks grew thin and weary trying to maintain the world as they had been. Darkness crept in at the corners, reclaiming space that had been stolen by this new realm. The emptiness, with its lonely cold, would come back. Rhiannon wanted to cry. This world that the light had made for them was so beautiful. How could it be so fragile?

But then, Rhiannon saw a burst of light, and she turned her eyes down to the sprawling world below. The sparks were popping, sending shimmering tendrils of themselves into the world. Something was happening where the tiny flecks of color touched the ground. She was so far away and above that it was hard to see, and Rhiannon felt like the world moved closer to her to give her a better view.

Creatures were crawling from the ground. They were living, breathing beings, each unique to the region and color that had birthed it. Rhiannon saw them begin to do with their claws and hands and tails what the sparks had done by pure magic. Something else was flying through the air as well, thin strings of color that seemed to wrap itself around the creatures and help them with their tasks. They lived in harmony with the land, a reflection of the dance the light had done before. It was perfect. As Rhiannon flew back out to see the whole of the world, she could see the populations of magnificent, surreal creatures following a life cycle in rapid speeds. Generation after generation of creature lived out their life and died peacefully, tending the land.

It was perfect. The golden light flowed around and through the creation, blissfully giving new and exciting growth to the world around them. Rhiannon felt completely at peace.

This is it, Rhiannon thought, realizing the pieces of the world she had just witnessed. The fey and the thread were creations of the Goddess, which were creations from The Source, and all things worked together to keep the precarious, ever flowing world in balance. The darkness was waiting on the edge, though. It was vital that the dance continue. All beings had their roles. *I understand,* Rhiannon said to herself, turning her attention back to her physical body. She had seen what she needed to. The Otherworld was beautiful. It made sense to her.

Rhiannon felt like she was being pulled up by a string, zooming out and away from the sight of the Otherworld's creation, until she could see nothing but darkness again. She became aware that her arms were asleep, filled with pinpricks.

"Rhiannon?"

Rhiannon opened her eyes.

Before her, a woman stood in the darkness, alone. Her wrists and ankles had metal cuffs around them, keeping her body held in a rigid X. The chains lead off into nothingness. She was draped in a dirty white cloth, a ragged hole cut for her head. Her bones showed through her skin, and the hair that Rhiannon remembered as a lustrous black mane was matted and dull. If it weren't for her eyes, Rhiannon would not have known her, but there was no mistaking her. It was her mother.

For a split second, Rhiannon remembered the dream she had when she'd arrived in this world, the cat with eyes just like these, and felt a cold grip in her stomach. *Funny what turns up when you go looking,* Grandma Deedee from her dream had said.

But it couldn't be her mother. Her mother had run off when she was eight, never calling or writing, but Rhiannon had always imagined her as a wild bohemian. This vision of her looked like she was in some medieval prison.

"Rhiannon! It is you! My little girl!" Her mother said. Her voice, melting with happiness, twisted something raw and painful in Rhiannon's gut.

"Mom..." Rhiannon managed. She took a step forward, then stopped. Rhiannon noticed the bruises and cuts on her mother's face. Strange marks had been etched into her arms and legs, wounds flowing between scabs and scars. This had been going on a long time. Everything else suddenly mattered a lot less.

"Mom, what's happened to you? Where are you?" Rhiannon surged forward, pushing through the darkness. It felt like swimming through drying concrete.

Suddenly her mother's expression turned anxious and she shook her head. "I. . . I'm sorry, I can't tell you," Her mother suddenly looked terrified. "You have to go. Rhiannon, stay back. Don't touch me!"

"Mom!" Rhiannon said, trying to move closer to her. There was something holding her back but she pushed against it. All reasoning hesitation was lost. This was her mother, in chains and bleeding. Nothing was going to stop her. "Mommy, wait! Let me help you! Mom!"

Her mother was shaking her head harder and harder, tears coming to her eyes. "I'm sorry, I'm sorry," She said. It sounded like her voice was fading away.

Rhiannon started screaming, desperate to be heard before her mother was gone. She ignored the cold creeping into her blood. She couldn't go, not yet. "Mom! Stop! Please, let me help you! Where are you? Where are you? Mom!"

She felt the cold pulling deeper on her stomach, dragging harder against her and as the image of her mother pulled further away. "Mom!" Rhiannon wailed.

"Rhiannon!" Martin's voice pierced the darkness and she opened her eyes again, this time back in the room. Rhiannon was sobbing, shaking hard.

Martin was holding her arms tightly, obviously trying to hold her down. Rhiannon thrashed against him. "Let me go! Let me go!" She demanded "Where is my mother? Where's Mom?" Rhiannon wailed, tears pouring down her red, snotty face. She did not care. She had to find her mother.

"Rhiannon, please!" Martin begged.

"Let me go!" Rhiannon screeched, planting both of her hands

onto Martin's chest. She had only meant to shove him off of her, but a blast of frigid wind erupted from her palms, forcing Martin back into the wall behind him. He slammed against it with a terrific thud.

Rhiannon immediately sobered, leaping to her feet. "Martin!" Rhiannon gibbered. "I'm so sorry! I don't know what happened. I don't know what I did. I'm so sorry."

Martin tried to gesture that he was alright, but the air had been knocked out of him and he was having a hard time saying anything.

"What happened?" He managed to croak.

How could Rhiannon answer that question? She sat back on the bed, staring at the floor. Every detail of her mother's mutilated body was etched in her memory, churning her stomach with fear and rage. "It was awful," Rhiannon said. "I don't understand why Una would show me something like that. Why would she show me that?"

Martin coughed loudly, pounding his chest. "I'm sorry, what?" Martin said, furrowing his brow. "What did she show you?"

"My mom! But not my mom, not how I remember her. She was chained up and she had been hurt. . . But she knew me," Rhiannon furrowed her brow, shaking her head. "I don't understand what it meant. It couldn't really be my Mom. . . could it?"

Martin didn't respond. He sprang up to Una's side, clutching the limp woman's hand. "Little light? My rainbow?" He asked, voice urgent even in its attempt at playfulness. "Una! Una, please, come back."

The girl was lying very still. Martin reached out and very gently touched her cheek. "Una, wake up, my love," Martin whispered, practically begging.

Una's eyes flashed open, two pits of black, and Martin's eyes immediately filled with darkness. His body jerked rigid. Rhiannon curled on herself, wanting to be brave and yet feeling too raw and naked to move. The cold snaked inside of her, trying to send comfort, and Rhiannon threw fire at it. She did not want comfort. She wanted answers.

When Martin gasped back into his own body, both sets of eyes returned to normal. Una's fluttered for a moment, and then fell shut. She was asleep again. Martin stared at her, then looked at Rhiannon, incapable of speech.

"Martin?" Rhiannon asked, pleadingly. "Martin, tell me, please. What is going on?"

"Rhiannon, something amazing," Martin said slowly. He was speaking so softly that Rhiannon found herself leaning close to hear. "A miracle. I could not have hoped for such luck."

He leaned down and kissed Una's forehead, then grabbed Rhiannon's wrist and half dragged her from the room. In a sudden burst of restraint, he closed the door quietly, then spun her to face him. He clasped both of her shoulders so tightly that it hurt. Rhiannon tried to yank out of his grasp but stopped at the tone of his voice.

"Rhiannon!" He said, exultant. "Tell me everything. Tell me every detail of what you saw, starting from the beginning. Ask me any questions you like! This changes absolutely everything!"

"Oh?" Came a question from behind them.

Martin snapped his gaze to Bona's curious and disapproving expression. "I too find myself curious. What's changed, Martin?"

Rhiannon was confused at the painfully tight squeeze Martin gave her before releasing her arms completely, resuming a position of relative nonchalance. "Bona, please, let me talk to the girl before we make any sort of announcement. It might be nothing! You know how Una's visions are. Often times they seem to be one thing and then turn out completely different, yes?"

"You seemed oddly certain," Bona insisted, folding his arms. "What happened?"

"I—" Rhiannon began.

"Rhiannon, stop!" Martin interjected. "Bona, I must refuse. This is too delicate. She is just beginning her training and—"

"It's about her mother, isn't it?" Bona growled, glaring. "You wouldn't sound like that if it wasn't about the girl's mother."

"Wait. . . *You* know about my mother?" Rhiannon asked. She felt like her insides were going to melt out of her body. It was impossible to believe, and yet here she was experiencing it. How did these fey know anything about Bridget O'Farrell?

"Child, we wouldn't be here right now if it wasn't for your mother," Bona replied. The venom that dripped off his words could've burned holes in the floorboards.

"Stop!" Martin commanded, glaring. "You must stop, Bona. Do not do this."

Bona opened his mouth angrily, but hesitated and closed it again with a sigh. The two stared at each other as though playing an invisible game of chess, and finally Bona shook his head.

"You are not your brother, Martin. Stop trying to act like him," and with that, the satyr turned away towards the stairs. He spoke without looking back. "We will vacate this house. I don't know what's going on, but if The Last Druid is involved we must take every precaution. You are, as always, welcome to come with us."

"Your hospitality is very kind," Martin said grimly, making Bona chuckle as he went down the stairs.

"Martin?" Rhiannon asked. There was an edge in her voice that it would be dangerous to ignore.

"Yes, yes. I'm sorry. It is a complicated story and. . . Well, Bona doesn't have all of the details. I cared deeply for your mother, we all did. When things went wrong, many people felt rather, well, betrayed." Martin shrugged.

"My mother was here?" It felt like a thousand hairline fractures were splitting through her brain and everything she knew was oozing out of them. "All this time. She's been here."

"Yes." Martin said warily. He was looking at a fragile, cracked thing that would shatter if the wind blew wrong, but he couldn't believe it was too late. "I'm sorry, Rhiannon. I know this is a shock."

Rhiannon gritted her teeth. She wanted to scream and smash things. She was having a hard time remembering why she shouldn't. "So, what, you guys just lied to us?" she shouted, "You and Grandma cooked up some scheme so that we wouldn't know our Mother had been taken to the land of the fairies? Or does Grandma even know?" Rhiannon yelped, suddenly horrified. How would she tell Grandma?

"She knows!" Martin assured her. "At least, she knows most of it."

Rhiannon gaped at him. "I thought you couldn't lie!"

"I can't! But there are times when I cannot tell certain truths." Martin said. Frustration and shame flushed his cheeks. "Rhiannon, I know how it seems, but you must understand; Everything, absolutely everything I do is for the protection of The Source, the world, and your family."

"Why?" Rhiannon demanded. "Why is my family caught up in all this?"

"I don't know, Rhiannon," Martin said sighing. "I've asked myself that thousands, millions of times, little love. Why the O'Farrells?

Why not another family or different families, to spread the burden? I care deeply for your clan, Rhiannon. I have been with you since your Grandmother was a baby! It hurts to see what's become of it because of us. But that's why I need you to tell me what you saw. I cannot give up on fixing this."

Rhiannon glared at him. She wanted to reject it, to call him a fraud and demand to be taken home immediately, but everything in her itched to see her mother again. The image of her mother in chains had changed something in her. An idea cracked over her head, sending shivers down her spine. It seemed completely obvious. There was only one way to be sure. "Okay," Rhiannon finally said, "but you must promise me something."

Martin's face went from pleading to warry in an instant. "Rhiannon, you do not want to make a bargain with a fey." He said quickly. "This will end poorly."

"I need this!" Rhiannon insisted, poking him in the chest perhaps a bit too hard. "I need to know that if I help you, we will save my mother. No more tricks, no more games. Promise me, and I'll do whatever you want."

Martin stared at her hard. Rhiannon watched his face. It seemed like the muscle over his eye was twitching.

"I do not accept." Martin finally spat the words through gritted teeth. He seemed to be fighting something. "I will not make a bargain with you."

Rhiannon glared, crossing her arms tightly. "Then I won't help you!" Rhiannon said. "Those are the terms. If you agree to help me save my mother, then I'll work with you and be cooperative and obedient. If not, then I'm not going to do anything."

Martin was trembling. He backed up from Rhiannon. "No!" Martin choked out the word and groaned in pain. He fell to his knees, hands flying to cradle his head as though trying to hold it in one piece. "I won't do it! I won't make another pact with them!" Martin said, turning his head upwards as though addressing someone above him.

"Why not?" Rhiannon demanded. She was flabbergasted. "I don't understand why you won't help me. It's my mother. You said you care about us!"

Martin turned in on himself, placing his forehead on his knees. "Rhiannon, fey bargains. . . Aaaaah!" He moaned, wrenching back in pain. He barred his teeth and practically growled at the sky. "I will tell her, you cursed noise! Fey bargains never end ho-ooooow!" His sentence was cut short by a wail of pain. He fell to his side.

Rhiannon reached out to help him but Martin jerked himself away, writhing in pain. "No! Don't touch me! It might consider it agreement!" Martin yelped.

"What might?" Rhiannon asked, baffled. He was acting like a man possessed. For all she knew, he could be.

"The music!" He managed to moan.

"Martin, I take it back!" Rhiannon tried, "I take it back. No bargains, no deals."

It stopped. Martin's body went limp. Panting heavily, he managed to turn his gaze to her and smiled. "Thank you, Rhiannon." He said softly, relief and gratitude dripping from every word. Then he said, almost observationally, "I've never been able to fight it off before."

"Martin. . . will you help me?" Rhiannon asked around the lump in her throat. She was also crying, but was trying very hard to ignore it. "I'm sorry for causing you so much trouble but I don't know how else to be sure. I need to be able to trust you."

"My elegant little tornado of doom," Martin said making Rhiannon grin in spite of herself, "I will help you. You do not need to offer me anything in exchange for it. I am honored to serve."

"Oh. Okay," Rhiannon said.

Downstairs, the house was a mess of activity. Ainsel, Cat, and Bona were packing everything. Bona went from room to room, opening sparkling green portals in the walls for easy transportation. Martin and Rhiannon struggled to stay out from underfoot as they talked.

"So, I think I understand everything. . ." Rhiannon said, "The Source made the world, then made Goddesses to look after it, but they couldn't keep up so the Goddesses made the fey."

"Good!" Martin said. "Now, the thread?"

"It's the energy leftover from the fey creation. Each fey is made of part of the Otherworld and part of the Goddess, but some of their power is left in the world, right?"

"Quite. You've been a quick study." Martin said happily.

"Martin, we need that sofa!" Bona chirped at them. They quickly stood to avoid being carted through the portal. There was no nonsense in the satyr's method and no time to waste for lollygagging. Martin and Rhiannon moved to sit on the steps.

"I still have questions, though." Rhiannon said.

"Fire away!"

"Why does everyone call Earth the void?"

"Easy. Fey can't travel there." Martin replied.

"Watch out!" Ainsel shrieked from the top of the stairs. Martin just managed to jerk Rhiannon out of the way of a case tumbling down the steps. Ainsel looked down at them with horrified shock.

"I'm so sorry!" She called.

"It's fine, dear heart," Martin replied, "Not a scratch on us. Let's go to the kitchen, shall we?"

As Martin lead Rhiannon through the mostly empty living room, she continued their conversation. "But that can't possibly be true! You travel there, after all."

"Haven't you realized by now that I'm not like most fey?"

Martin drawled. He gave her a grin that belonged on a movie poster from the 60s.

"In that you're far more annoying? Yes, I have noticed." Rhiannon said, but there was no venom in her words. "So why can you go there and nobody else?"

The kitchen was tiny and there was nowhere to sit, so Rhiannon jumped up to perch on the counter. Martin rummaged through the pantry and made a noise of delight when he found a kettle. "Look! We can have tea! If there's tea. . ." He realized.

"Martin?" Rhiannon pressed, stretching out a leg to poke him with her toe. He sighed and looked up from the kettle.

"Yes, yes. Alright. I can travel to Earth because my Goddess sent all of her thread there. In fact, I must return to Earth every so often or I start to turn a little mangy. Fey can't exist without their thread and their land from which they were made. That's why all the other fey that travel to Earth lose their substance and I do not. To them it's a void. To me it's my home," He turned back to the cupboard and his search for tea.

"So who is your Goddess, anyway? Goddess of Smug Pretention?"

"Ha. Ha. You funny little stoat." Martin paused his rummaging to smile at her. "No, sorry dear. That's not relevant to saving your mom and I still have some obligations to keep. You'll have to wait on that one."

"What if I guess it?" Rhiannon tried.

"Not even if you guess it," Martin pouted as he turned up yet another empty drawer. "I know I brought them back some tea the last time. . . If only you hadn't whisked us away so suddenly I could've restocked. Ah well."

"Well, we'll be going home soon anyway, right?" Rhiannon shrugged.

Martin froze for the briefest moment, but covered it relatively well. "Really? Here I was thinking we were off to save your mother?" Martin said cheerfully.

Rhiannon hesitated. "Well yes. . . We are, of course, but can't we go home first?"

Martin stopped again and turned back to her, not bothering to hide his concern. "Rhiannon, I swear, I truly am sorry for how all this has gone. There were many things that happened, things that have nothing to do with you, that have lead us to this place. I would've much rather taught you all of these things gradually, and given you a chance to understand your powers before I asked—"

"Martin! There you are!" Bona snapped, swinging open the kitchen door. "We're closing the house down. You need to go through a portal, quickly. Hop to!"

"You were going to leave without the kettle!" Martin said. He waved the metal pot in outrage. "Aren't you glad I was here to save it? Why, these things are expensive, you know."

"Yes, yes, very well done," Bona sighed, waving them through the door. The living room was stripped bare, every book and footstool gone. Bona pointed at the wall and a green circle crackled into existence, revealing another living room.

"Go on, now," Bona said, shooing them towards it. "I've got to be the last one through, you know."

Martin strolled through the circle without so much as batting an eye. Rhiannon was a bit more cautious, but stumbled through without a hitch. Her mouth tasted of lime for a split second and then she was standing on plush, cream colored carpet. A fire crackled in a large fireplace. Cat was putting books into a shelf and Ainsel was running from room to room shrieking in delight.

"Wow," Rhiannon said. She was genuinely impressed.

"Yes, Bona is the backbone of the resistance in many ways," Martin said. Rhiannon looked at him suspiciously, much to his confusion. "What?"

"You hate him!" Rhiannon whispered.

"I do not!" Martin protested. "I find him to be frustrating at times, but the same could be said for you, little wolverine."

Rhiannon smiled. She could get used to this new version of pet-names. "Wait, the resistance?" Rhiannon said, her ears catching up with her brain. "What are you guys resisting, then?"

"The High Council, of course," Bona said from behind them.

"Really?" Martin chimed, "You're resisting them again? Here I was thinking that you'd curled up and become their little lap goat!"

Bona was not amused by his comment. He sighed stiffly through his nose. "Martin, just because we don't all want to burn the world down and rebuild from scratch does not mean that those of us who show restraint support those buffoons."

Martin grinned. "All I needed was to hear you call them buffoons."

"So, why are they the bad guys?" Rhiannon asked.

"Martin, I suppose I'll allow you to take this one. I have to go insure that the wards are secure. If you'll excuse me, Druid," He said. There was only the tiniest bit of sarcasm in the bow he gave her and Rhiannon supposed that she could forgive him that. She would probably have been equally snippy in his position.

But Martin's pensive face made her suspicious. "What?" Rhiannon asked.

"Well I was thinking. . . Perhaps it'd be easiest to explain what we're doing this for if I just showed you," Martin offered.

Cat looked up from his work and frowned at them. "Martin, don't get her killed. I like her."

"Nothing like that!" Martin exclaimed, "I just feel that it's something easier observed than explained, wouldn't you agree?"

"This is the problem that you need me to fix?" Rhiannon asked.

"Well, I feel that you're the most likely candidate. . . see, it must be a Druid. The High Council thinks that the solution to the problem is chaining up your mother and using her as a sort of patch to hold the world together, but—"

"What?" Rhiannon shrieked. Cat leaped onto his hands and legs, and Bona and Ainsel scurried into the room.

"What happened?" Bona blustered.

"They're using *my mom?*" The rage inside of Rhiannon could've melted lead.

"Yes, and it's not working." Martin said, unmoved. "Do you want to see for yourself?"

. . .

The journey was much longer than it had been the first time Rhiannon had flown. Martin had been difficult and esoteric about where they were headed, but had simply asked The North Wind to take them to see the place that was its home. They had traveled away from Hub in the opposite direction of the jungle that Rhiannon had arrived in, and she wondered for a moment how big the Otherworld really was. It seemed to stretch forever.

To pass time, she tried to chat with the wind.

Why did you leave your home, then? Rhiannon asked.

The Devastation came. The wind replied stiffly.

What's the Devastation?

The wind bristled. *Isn't that the whole reason for this voyage? So that you can see for yourself? Not that I was consulted in the wisdom of this choice.*

Rhiannon didn't want to leave it alone. *So like. . . what made the Devastation come? And how am I supposed to stop it?*

The wind begrudgingly cooperated. *The Otherworld is built of many parts, all of which rely on one another. If any one part crumbles, the rest cannot survive. My fey left their land and we could not keep the magic sated alone. It needed more than the thread could provide.*

Then why would they leave? Rhiannon asked, disbelieving.

They seemed to think The High Council was making it worth their while. The wind refused to speak any more, carrying Rhiannon forward through blurring landscape at an impossible speed. Although the silence was disappointing, it wasn't as though she was bored. The world she was in was much bigger and much more beautiful than she had imagined before, and seeing the different regions passing beneath her kept her occupied.

And then, all of a sudden, the land flattened out. It was strange, as though someone had simply come in with a rolling pin and smoothed out the wrinkles of rugged terrain and left a flat sheet in its place. Bits of scrub scattered across the plain, but they were scraggly and devoid of life. The wind circled wide and high, showing that this tundra expanded for miles.

This is it. The wind said.

Rhiannon was not surprised so much as confused. *What's so dangerous about this place?* She asked. *It just seemed like it's empty. How is that harmful?*

Just wait. The wind replied. The power felt taut and jagged, like a bird who could sense a predator nearby even if it couldn't see it yet.

It was eerie and quiet, as though there were a muffling blanket over the world. Time stretched out, slower than it should be. Rhiannon realized that the feeling of tense anxiety was not limited to the wind but included the land around her. Nothing moved. Nothing breathed. Everything felt like fear.

What's going on? Rhiannon finally asked when she felt like the dread inside of her would swallow her whole.

Almost. . . The wind hissed.

And then Rhiannon saw it. There was a shiver, on the horizon, a teaming and shimmering light, growing and bubbling. The wind jerked back, already flowing away from the light as it approached. Rhiannon looked back, watching in horror at what was happening.

The billowing light razed the land, ripping and shredding the tiny shrubs to pieces. It raged along, reaching across the space of the horizon, gobbling everything that it touched. The wind dashed and darted ahead of it, but Rhiannon wanted to scream. She could see the delicate branches of the plants being ripped asunder, the shards that remained dissolving into light until nothing was left.

The light was gaining on them. Rhiannon realized that even in the body of her cold she could feel the heat of the light's consumption, feel the real fear that the wind felt as it moved as quick as it could.

Go! Rhiannon begged the wind. She pushed her own energy behind the power of cold, doing everything she could to throw herself away from the light that seemed to be gaining on them. Rhiannon channeled all the fire and passion she could, and the wind surged away, managing to outrun the light. Rhiannon kept pushing, feeding all of herself into the thread, sending them reeling farther and farther away. All she could think of was surviving, escaping. Long after the flat lands had been replaced by forest and mountains, Rhiannon kept running.

Fleshling! The cold called to her, but she did not stop.

Rhiannon, please! The cold screamed, desperate.

Rhiannon could not stop. She was so afraid, so desperate to get away and get to safety that it did not occur to her that she was running out of fire. There had to be more somewhere, didn't there? Rhiannon reached deeper into herself, pulling out more power. She had to get away, she had to save herself.

Stop! Screeched the cold, suddenly yanking Rhiannon back to the physical world. Rhiannon's limbs flailed as she hurtled through the air at speed. There was a horrible, suspended moment as the ground raced beneath her. She tried to pull her arms up and shield her face, but the wind around her was rushing too fast. This was going to kill her, she realized. She winced against the coming impact.

She was enveloped in a mountain of freezing, wet snow, cushioning her fall. She was still wearing the completely useless dress she'd borrowed from Ainsel and her arms and legs were covered in scrapes.

Be glad that's all that hurts! The cold snapped viciously.

Rhiannon dragged herself out of the snow. Martin was nearby, extracting himself from the already melting snowdrift with less success. His skin looked slightly blue.

"D-do you need help?" Rhiannon stammered, thankful that the climate they were in seemed to be too warm for the snow. It looked like a temperate forest of some sort. Martin seemed to nod and Rhiannon came to pull him free.

You nearly burned yourself out! The power hollered at her, refusing to be ignored. *It was all I could do to stop you! What were you thinking, putting your life magic into me that way? That's how we kill the stupid fey who seek to destroy us! You must never do that again!*

Rhiannon winced at the blaring lecture between her ears. Her hand pressed against her forehead where it felt like an icepick was driving through her cranium. "I swear! I'm sorry!" she said desperately. The power backed off slightly, but Rhiannon could feel that it was still furious with her, still scared for itself. It was not remotely comforting.

Martin gently touched the top of her head and Rhiannon looked up at him. He's expression was simply concerned and curious. "You're alright, then?" He suggested.

She stepped in to hug him, putting her stinging arms around his chest. She didn't care if it was weird. She just really wanted a hug.

Martin awkwardly wrapped his arms around her, holding her. To his horror her shoulder were shaking, but he told himself that it was just the cold. Then he heard her sniffling into his coat. Rhiannon was crying? "Rhi?" He said, putting a hand on top of her head.

She tilted her head back and looked at him, face red and blotchy from cold and crying. "I thought it was going to get me, Martin!" She squeaked, voice thin and high from barely restrained emotion. "I thought I was going to die! I was so scared." The tears bubbled up in her eyes and she buried her head back in his coat.

Martin's heart shattered. He held her tightly, letting her sob. He felt utterly useless in this moment. He hunched at the shoulders so that she could lean into his shoulder and he wrapped his arms around her as tightly as he could. "It's okay now," Martin said, wondering how much that little truth meant. "I understand it's too much. . . I'm sorry. I thought that this was the easiest way to explain. I'll take you home now, Rhiannon. I made a mistake."

"No!" Rhiannon said, wrenching back from him. Martin blinked at her scowling face in surprise. "No, I'm not going home. Not yet. First, we fix this."

"Rhiannon, you don't have to-" Martin began, but Rhiannon interrupted him by punching him in the shoulder. It didn't hurt, but the shock of it stopped him abruptly. They stared at eachother. Tears still rolled down her face and her shoulders shook with sobs forced back, but she glared at him viciously.

"Martin, I do have to!" Rhiannon's words were all but growled. "You said that they were keeping my mom here because of this, and that I can make it stop. Well, then I'm going to fix it."

"Rhiannon, your family. Your grandmother and brothers. . . " Martin tried gently. He tried not to wince in anticipation of more punches, but Rhiannon did not strike again. She simply shook her head.

"I know! I know, I know, but I'm not thinking about that right now." Rhiannon snapped. "Martin, after all this time I want my mother back. I want to have a mom and I won't leave without her. Tell me how to fix this so that she can come home."

Martin fell to his knees, wrapping Rhiannon in an embrace of gratitude and exhaustion. "Thank you," Martin whispered. "Thank you, Rhiannon."

Rhiannon held him, letting her head fall into the crook of his shoulder. She had grown up without parents, and she wondered if this was what it felt like to be held by a father. It was nice. It couldn't last.

Martin let her go and quickly wiped his cheeks with his sleeve, the wet cloth smearing his tears more than drying them. "Sorry. I've been waiting for someone to help for a long time, you see. . ."

"It's cool." Rhiannon said quickly, trying to grin at him. They chuckled awkwardly, breaking the emotional tension. Rhiannon took a deep breath, bracing herself. "Martin, the wind told me a lot of things, but. . . it sounds like I'm going to have to do a lot of magic. Will you teach me how to work with the thread? How to do it properly so that the land will be okay?"

He smirked at her. "Yes, dear little migraine. I absolutely will."

"Great," Rhiannon said, "What do we do first?"

Martin sprang to his feet, coming to life. "The first step is to return to the safety of Bona's secret base. From there, we'll travel the Otherworld and tame the thread. You have more talent than anyone I've ever met, but you need to learn control."

"And if we do that then my mom will be free?"

Martin hesitated, pulling a wince. "Well, yes. . ."

"Martin, tell me." Rhiannon demanded.

The gangly fey held on to the information for a moment, as though weighing his options, but relented in a gush. "Your mother has been captive to them for years and very few fey know exactly what sorts of magic she's been made to do. I have asked a thousand questions, found out everything that I can, but even now all I know is that she is their answer to the Devastation that's happening all over the Otherworld. She is supposed to use her magic to encompass all of the plains that are empty and feed it enough of herself to support it, even without fey living there."

Rhiannon's mind reeled at the size of the task. "But that's impossible! How could they think that would work?"

"The fey have forgotten where they came from. . ." Martin said sadly.

"But you haven't," Rhiannon pointed out, "and Una hasn't! Why can't you just tell them the truth?"

Martin gave her a bitter look. "You think I'm not trying?"

"Right." Rhiannon said, sheepish. Of course Martin would try. That was silly of her. She took a deep breath. "So, if I do this, then my mother will be saved, right?"

Martin nodded, but grimaced. "Rhiannon, I must tell you,

there are no guarantees with this. We will do our best. We will try everything in our power to save her, and the world, but it isn't going to fall into our laps. It is going to take time."

"Sure. So, like a week?" Rhiannon said.

Martin raised a dry eyebrow at her and shook his head again. Gravity sank on Rhiannon and she wondered how long it would be. She thought about Grandma. She thought of Bear, Jenny, and Colin. She thought about her favorite hiding spot in the backyard. She thought about her mother, and her jaw clinched. She had to do it. She was sorry, but she had to do it. Her life would just have to wait.

"Alright. Then we should probably get started, huh?" She said.

Martin grinned. "Yes, I think we should."

End of Book One

From the Author

Dear Reader,

I put a lot of stock in words, but I don't know how to describe how cool this moment is. I wrote this, and you are reading it. It all feels a little magical from my point of view. If you skipped ahead to the end, that's alright! I'm still glad you picked the book up. Thank you.

This is my first book and not my last. Many people would not forgive me for the precipice I have allowed you all to dangle off of if I stopped here. Trust me, I know. Rhiannon has a much bigger adventure ahead of her. This is just the beginning.

As a writer, I always hope that the author notes will contain a secret that will help me with my own creative struggle. Of course, I can only speak for my own process, but here's what worked for me. I decided I was going to write whatever I had, even if it was trash, and didn't stop working until it was done. I didn't get mad at myself for writing something terrible or hide when I didn't know what I was doing. I just kept going. Eventually, it turned into a book. So, for those of you who are mucking through your own creative swamp, that's what I can give you. Keep going and do not let anger or fear get in your way, regardless of if you're writing a novel, baking a cake, or trying to save the world of the fairies from imminent destruction.

You can follow along with the progress of my next book at **www.patreon.com/speegs** and see my process of writing in real time. Again, thank you for picking this up and sharing this with me. It has been my pleasure.

Love,

Erica Speegle

Made in the USA
Las Vegas, NV
25 February 2021